PENGUIN METRO READS

BAD LIARS

Vikrant Khanna is a captain in the merchant navy and the bestselling author of *Secretly Yours*, *The Girl Who Knew Too Much* and *The Girl Who Disappeared*. He lives and works in Singapore.

bad liars

ONE MURDER.

THREE LIARS.

VIKRANT KHANNA

BESTSELLING AUTHOR OF
THE GIRL WHO KNEW TOO MUCH

Penguin
metro reads

An imprint of Penguin Random House

PENGUIN METRO READS

USA | Canada | UK | Ireland | Australia
New Zealand | India | South Africa | China

Penguin Metro Reads is part of the Penguin Random House group of companies
whose addresses can be found at global.penguinrandomhouse.com

Published by Penguin Random House India Pvt. Ltd
4th Floor, Capital Tower 1, MG Road,
Gurugram 122 002, Haryana, India

First published in Penguin Metro Reads by Penguin Random House India 2023

10 9 8 7 6 5 4 3 2 1

ISBN 9780143459132

Typeset in Sabon by Manipal Technologies Limited, Manipal
Printed at Thomson Press India Ltd, New Delhi

www.penguin.co.in

Contents

Prologue

Sanya wakes up with a start and sits upright on her bed, almost motionless for a few minutes. Her neck feels stiff, and she gently caresses it with her right hand. She looks outside the bedroom window to her left. The morning is crisp and bright. The first rays of sunlight light up the room. Tiny motes of dust dance it as it slants through the window on to the carpeted floor across from the bed.

She closes her eyes, inhales deeply and begins concentrating on her breath. She meditates for the next fifteen minutes, oblivious to her surroundings—a morning routine that she has religiously followed for as long as she can remember. When she is done, she gets off the bed and walks over to the dresser.

She sits down on a chair and looks at her reflection in the mirror. A tired face looks back at her. At thirty, she should be looking younger, she thinks. Her hair has already started greying, albeit just a few strands on the left side of her head. She notices a few pimples dotting her cheeks and runs a lazy hand over them. She leans forward and examines the dark circles under her eyes, not inordinately concerned. She hasn't been sleeping well over the past few weeks.

She had turned thirty last month and, on her insistence, her husband had thrown a lavish party at their sprawling bungalow in Golf Links, Gurgaon. Her rich and famous husband is a real scrooge and hates parting with his money.

A smile escapes her at the memory of the silly argument she had had with him. It had taken her weeks to convince him that it was okay to spend money on special occasions. She turns her head to the left and lifts her hair to expose the scalp. The round Band-Aid doesn't quite cover the entire wound on her brow and a small patch of skin, with dried blood on it, has escaped its confines. She runs a soft hand over it and gently presses it. She winces in pain and leaves it alone.

She puts on her glasses and rises, her eyes still on the mirror. She is tall, just a few inches shy of six feet. She looks piercingly into her own eyes for a minute or two, before heading to the bathroom.

After her morning rituals, she steps out of her bedroom and heads downstairs to the kitchen.

Their helper, Sharda, greets her with an affable smile.

'Hello, Sanya madam.'

'How are you, Sharda? All good?'

Sharda nods. 'I'll get you some tea. Breakfast is almost ready, just a few more minutes.'

'Sure, thanks.'

Sharda then gazes at her forehead and, in a flash, her face puckers in a frown. 'What happened, madam?' she points at the Band-Aid.

Sanya hisses sharply through her teeth. Sharda is looking intently at her. 'I . . . I fell from . . .' she stops. 'I think you already know, Sharda.'

Sharda looks at her pityingly, 'Oh, madam, he hit you again, didn't he?' Then adds after a pause, 'Was it after dinner when he was, er . . . scolding you?'

'Yes,' Sanya says. 'When we went upstairs to our room.'

'But why do you let him, madam?'

Sanya doesn't reply. Sharda is looking at her expectantly waiting for an answer. When her gaze doesn't drop, Sanya says helplessly, 'You wouldn't understand, Sharda. It's not that easy.'

Sharda wants to add a rebuttal, but her eyes fall on the gas stove, and she hurriedly turns off the flame. Some tea boils over from the saucepan. She mops up the mess and pours the tea into two cups. The toaster behind her produces a loud ding and she extracts the bread slices and places them on a plate. She retrieves the butter from the refrigerator.

'Okay madam, you take the tea. I'll lay out breakfast on the table shortly.' She looks up at the wall clock. 'It's not even seven. You're up early today.'

Sanya yawns. 'Yes, I couldn't sleep well last night.'

Sharda nods slowly, obviously concerned, as she butters the toast. 'Where is sir?'

'I'm not sure,' she replies, shaking her head. 'Haven't you seen him yet? He's an early riser.'

'No,' Sharda replies. 'I haven't seen him since morning.'

'Okay, he might be in his study in the basement then,' Sanya says, 'reading something.' She rolls her eyes. 'He just reads all the time. Sometimes I think he's a book with two legs sticking out.'

Sharda lets out a hearty laugh and Sanya chuckles, breaking the tension in the air.

'Okay, let me go and call him.'

'Sure, madam.' Then as an afterthought, she adds, 'Don't let him do this to you. Men become stronger when they know their women need them.'

Sanya takes the stairs down on the left of the kitchen and calls out her husband's name. Once. Twice. It doesn't take long for her to cover the entire length of the basement. At the far end, she pushes the door to her husband's study.

She screams.

PART—1

MURDER. INITIAL INVESTIGATION. ARREST

ONE

Hearing Sanya's ear-splitting scream, Sharda comes sprinting down the stairs. Both women clap their hands over their mouth, and a sharp squeal escapes Sharda.

They stare at the corpse of Sanya's husband, Anant Kapoor. The body is spreadeagled on the floor beside the desk, in a pool of blood. There is a deep gash on the left side of the head. A blue vase, probably the murder weapon, lies a few inches away.

Sharda moves forward to pick it up.

'Don't!' Sanya stops her. 'It could—it could be . . . evid . . . evidence.'

Sanya is breathing heavily now. The hair on her arm stand on end. She feels a thin film of sweat at the back of her neck. She turns to Sharda.

'Call the police! Call the police!' she splutters. 'Oh my God! Oh my God!'

And then the tears come streaming down. With a choked sob, she bends over the corpse. She reaches out her right hand, wanting to touch him, but then holds back and clenches her hand into a fist.

Sharda picks the telephone from the desk and dials 100.

A police jeep screeches to a halt outside 23, Golf Links. A tall, well-built man and a short woman with curly, black hair, both in police uniform, step out. The man has a strong jaw, neat, cropped hair and sinewy, athletic arms; his uniform fits him perfectly. He removes his sunglasses and slips them into his shirt pocket. Her pudgy frame makes the woman look shorter than she really is; she has sharp, piercing eyes and an air of self-assurance in her gait.

They walk towards the bungalow, past the neatly manicured front lawn and past the yellow-and-black crime-scene tape pinned outside the door.

Inside the house, the atmosphere is dark and solemn. The curtains in the hall are still drawn and the air smells musty. Two police officers to their left in the living room are questioning a young man and a weeping woman who are seated on a giant beige leather sofa. They pause to glance around and, after a quick nod to their fellow officers, head past the dining hall and take the stairs down to the basement.

Downstairs, they turn left and head towards the room at the far end. The door is ajar, and they step into the study of the deceased man.

The forensics team is quietly going about their job, clicking photographs of the dead body and collecting evidence.

'Hello. I am inspector Danish Maurya, crime branch, east zone, in charge of the case.' He nods towards his female colleague. 'This is sub-inspector Kiran.'

A bald, middle-aged man steps forward, 'I am Desai from forensics.' He looks over his shoulder at the dead body. 'We'll be sending the body for autopsy soon, but from the looks of it, it appears to be very straightforward. That blue copper vase,' he points to his colleague with the latex gloves, who is packing and marking it, 'is the murder weapon and the victim was hit extremely hard just once. Death should have occurred in an instant due to major frontal impact.'

Maurya nods slowly. 'Do you have an estimate of the time of death?'

'Yes,' Desai replies, 'but very roughly. As per our preliminary forensic analysis it should be anywhere between 10 p.m. last night and 2 a.m. this morning. But after the autopsy, as death has occurred very recently, we should be able to narrow down that to . . . say, less than two hours by examining the state of the digestion of food.'

'Good,' Maurya says appreciatively. 'Please also let me know once you have the fingerprints off that vase.'

He steps towards the body and sits on his haunches. He studies the dead man. Late thirties or so, Maurya guesses.

'There wasn't any struggle before he died,' he tells Desai, pointing at the dead man's hands.

'Yes,' Desai agrees. 'It was a pop, and he was out.'

Maurya looks down again. The gash on the left side of the corpse's head is about an inch deep, exposing the skull. 'Whoever hit him, hit him hard,' he says to Kiran who is now hunkering down beside him.

'Yes, I agree,' she says. 'Must have hated him.'

'Well, let's find out.'

TWO

They head upstairs towards the hall and, after introducing themselves to Sanya and another thirty-something hefty man, sit down on the sofa.

'I'll take it from here,' Maurya gestures to the two police officers who had started their preliminary investigation. They nod and leave.

Maurya regards the woman, now a widow, in front of him. She appears visibly shattered and is shaking her head in disbelief. Her eyes are bloodshot and puffy, and tears still sparkle on her eyelashes. She is tall and pleasant-looking, and is still in her nightgown.

'I am very sorry for your loss, Mrs Kapoor,' he starts hesitantly and then clears his throat, 'but . . . er . . . I need to ask some questions.'

'Do we have to do it now?' the man seated beside Sanya says irritably.

Maurya now fixes his gaze on him. The thickset man, also in his nightclothes, is overweight, his pyjamas failing to disguise his protruding paunch. He looks tired like he hasn't slept all night. 'I'm sorry, and who are you?'

'I am Vicky. Anant's younger brother.'

'Do you live in this house?'

'Yes.' He nods and with a bored gesture indicates the corridor, 'On this floor. First room to the left.'

Maurya extracts a diary from the back pocket of his trousers. 'Can you tell me where you were last night between 10 p.m. and 2 a.m.?'

Vicky mutters under his breath. He doesn't hide his indignation and lets out an angry puff. 'I was with some friends in south Delhi, in a bar.'

Maurya makes a note in his diary. 'I see. And what time did you return home?'

Vicky shifts nervously on the sofa. Kiran notices a bead of sweat form on his forehead. He wipes it with the back of his hand. 'Around midnight. No, around 1 a.m.'

'Midnight or 1 a.m.?'

'1 a.m., 1 a.m.,' Vicky replies confidently this time. 'And then I just headed to my room and fell asleep in an instant. I drank too much last night.'

'I will need the contact details of your friends from last night.'

'Sure. No problem.'

Maurya turns to Sanya. 'Mrs Kapoor, can I ask you the same question? Where were you last night . . . same time?'

'In my bedroom.'

'You didn't step out of your room at all?'

'No.' Sanya sniffles and rubs her eyes with a handkerchief.

Maurya points at her forehead. 'What happened? How did you injure yourself?'

Sanya takes a deep breath. She steals a quick sidelong glance at Vicky, who nods back imperceptibly. Kiran, quick as a whip, perceives the subtle exchange.

Maurya waits for an answer impatiently, glancing back and forth between the two of them.

Sanya wipes her eyes again. 'My husband, he . . . he . . . er . . . hit me.'

Maurya leans forward and folds his arms across his chest. Kiran, beside him, raises her eyebrows. She is also drawn to the edge of her seat. She stares wide-eyed at Sanya.

'When?'

'Last night.'

Maurya and Kiran look at each other pensively for a quick moment, before Maurya turns back to Sanya. 'Okay, but what time?'

'After dinner,' she replies, looking at the wall clock in front of her. 'We had dinner around 8 p.m., went upstairs to our bedroom, and . . . and . . .' she stops, and tears stream afresh from her eyes. 'I'm sorry, but what has this got to do with the case? My husband and I quarrelled often, as married couples invariably do.'

Maurya nods sympathetically. 'Yes, yes, I understand. But, you see, right after your fight, he was murdered. So, we need to know what happened.'

Now, Sanya huffs angrily. 'I . . . I think it was around 8 p.m. We were arguing over dinner and then in our room; the spat got out of control. He pushed me—I don't think he meant to—and I crashed into the mirror. He was very apologetic afterwards.'

'I see.' Maurya makes a note. He looks up. 'And has this happened in the past? I mean the physical abuse, did he hit—'

'Please, inspector,' Vicky interrupts him sharply. 'My brother was a good man. Do not defame him!'

Maurya sits back in his chair and throws out his arms in protest. He regards Vicky in disdain. 'I just asked a simple question.'

'Yes, inspector. He did hit me a few times,' Sanya replies evenly.

Maurya bites his lower lip and smiles coyly at Vicky, almost gloating, before turning back to Sanya. 'Were those mistakes as well or did he hit you on purpose?'

Vicky doesn't reply this time and looks at his sister-in-law earnestly.

'I . . . I don't know,' Sanya says. 'There's no easy answer. Sometimes he would get very angry and lose control. He was very irascible, you see. But he would always apologize later and make it up to me. Other than that, he was a very good husband. Like I said, all married couples fight. Please don't make it a big deal of this, because it isn't.' She sounds calmer this time.

Maurya nods thoughtfully. He contemplates querying her further on this topic, then decides against it. 'Anybody else living in this house?'

'Yes, our helper, Sharda. But she has gone out to run some errands.'

'Does she work here full time? Does she live here?'

'Yes,' Sanya replies. 'She has a room behind the kitchen.'

'Okay. I can speak to her later.' He turns to Kiran and nods. They both rise. 'Sorry,' he looks back at Sanya. 'One more question before we leave. Your husband was hit by a heavy object. He must have screamed. Didn't any of you hear him?'

'No,' Sanya replies, shaking her head slowly. 'He was in the basement. Our bedroom is on the first floor and diagonally opposite the study. I heard nothing, unfortunately, otherwise I would've rushed down.'

'And you discovered the dead body in the morning, right?'

'Yes, around 7. Sharda was with me as well.'

'Okay.' He turns to Vicky. 'And you didn't hear anything either?'

'No. Like I said, I was too drunk and passed out the instant I hit the bed.'

Too convenient, Maurya thinks.

'Okay, okay. Sure.' He drums his fingers on the cover of his diary, his mind still in overdrive. 'Is there anything else you'd like to share with us? Did anything unusual happen yesterday? Did he have, er . . . any enemies?'

'No.' Sanya shakes her head. 'Not that I am aware of.'

Vicky shakes his head mechanically.

'Do you suspect anybody?'

Both shake their heads again.

'Okay, thank you.' Before leaving, he jots down the name and telephone number of Vicky's friend from last night—his alibi.

When Maurya and Kiran are almost at the door, Sanya calls out from behind, 'Inspector, I forgot to tell you, but last night we had a visitor.'

Maurya's curiosity piqued, he turns around. *Why didn't she mention this earlier?*

'Mahesh Murthy,' Sanya continues. 'He was a friend of Anant, in fact they were business partners. He was here around 9 p.m., but I'm not sure when he left.'

Maurya jots down his telephone number as well, before heading out the door with Kiran.

THREE

They get in the jeep and fasten their seat belts. Maurya puts on his sunglasses, lowering his head to take in the view of the bungalow through the windshield. It is a big, beautiful, two-storeyed building, freshly painted in ivory and grey. There is a spacious car-parking area to the left that could easily house four cars. He spots the latest model of Mercedes convertible and a red Porsche and emits a wolf whistle.

'What do you think, Kiran? Do you believe her?'

'About what?'

'Those tears,' he says. 'More like crocodile tears. Did she look devastated at her husband's death?'

Kiran ponders this for a minute or two. 'Cannot say. Everybody reacts differently to tragedies. She was definitely shaken.'

'And the brother? He was sweating like a pig. It's November, for God's sake!'

'Hmm . . . he's a tricky one. A sly bastard if you ask me.' She turns to Maurya, 'And did you notice that subtle nod, that exchange between them, when you asked about the injury?'

'Yes, yes,' Maurya says animatedly, 'what was that? Was she taking his permission?'

'I don't know. Are they having an affair?'

Maurya smiles. 'Well, that's very . . . creative.'

'Why so?'

Maurya chuckles this time and nudges her with a salacious grin. 'Come on, Kiran, that lady with that fatso? Doesn't make any sense at all.'

'Well, love doesn't have to make sense.'

They head east in the jeep along National Highway 8 towards Cyber Hub. They have decided to meet Mahesh Murthy in his office. Kiran had given him a quick call to apprise him of their impending visit. He sounded relaxed, almost as though he had been expecting the call.

The ride is smooth along the wide expressway, and they reach their destination in less than fifteen minutes. Maurya parks the jeep right in front of the building and they head inside. They take the elevator to the twelfth floor and enter the first room on their left. The young receptionist rises and greets them in deference. She immediately pings her boss on the intercom, informing him of his visitors.

Mahesh Murthy is with them in a minute. He is a short, bespectacled man with thick, curly hair and is wearing an expensive suit. He ushers them into the office and guides them to his cabin. Inside his room, with a sharp jerk he draws the blinds to the windows which overlook the entire office and sits down on a chair behind a huge mahogany desk. Maurya and Kiran take their seat across from him.

'Yes, inspector,' he says disarmingly, 'what can I do for you?'

Maurya clears his throat. 'How did you know Anant Kapoor?'

Maurya notices that Mahesh does not flinch. *So, he is aware of the murder of his friend.*

'He was a good friend,' replies Mahesh. 'We worked together in the same investment company, Fidelity Group, for about six, seven years. And then we became business partners and started our own company about three years ago.' He shakes his head. 'But we parted ways last year.'

'I see. And why was that?'

Mahesh leans back in his chair and doesn't respond immediately. He thinks for a few moments, gazing at his two guests in turn. Then he sits upright again. 'See, it's complicated. We had started a PMS a few years—' When he gets puzzled looks from his visitors, he clarifies, 'Portfolio Management Service. We invest our clients' money and earn a commission on the amount invested, and a share of the returns if we exceed expectations. But after a few months, we realized that both of us had different strategies and it was getting difficult for us to work together. So, he sold his share to me and started his own PMS, primarily following the tenets of value investing—you know, buying companies below their intrinsic worth.'

Maurya sighs and ignores the financial jargon. 'And what is your strategy?'

Mahesh chuckles softly. 'Well, I . . . I'm an opportunist. I invest wherever I can make money. No rules for me.'

'Okay, sure,' Maurya says. 'And why were you meeting him yesterday?'

'Just catching up. We hadn't met in a long time.'

'When did you go into that house and what time were you out?'

Mahesh looks up at the ceiling, linking his hands behind his head. He closes his eyes and tries to recall. Then he looks at the inspector, leans forward to fold his arms on his desk and replies, 'I was there around 9 p.m. and I left about two hours later, around 11 p.m.'

Maurya makes a note in his diary. 'Did anybody see you leave at that time? Mrs Kapoor or their helper, for example?'

Mahesh shakes his head. 'No, why?'

'Because he died immediately after you left him!'

The colour drains from Mahesh's face now and he stiffens in his seat. Two pair of eyes are gazing at him with morbid intensity, slicing through to his very soul, and he feels extremely insecure in his own office. He swallows hard and realizes his throat is parched. He reaches for the glass of water beside him on a small table and gulps it down in one go.

'But—b . . . but . . .' he stutters nervously, 'I . . . I have an alibi.'

Maurya and Kiran exchange confused glances.

'Did I ask you that?' Maurya asks turning back to Mahesh. His voice is now steely and has lost the congenial undertone of a few minutes ago. His expression is an icy glare. 'Why would you say that? Did you *plan* an alibi?'

Mahesh notices the inspector's jaw stiffen and a nerve on his forehead visibly throbs. He realizes that he must weigh his words now. 'Sorry, I . . . I got carried away. Please call my friend, Joe. He lives down the same street, second last bungalow. After I left Anant's house, I was with him for the next hour.'

'Perfect,' says Maurya, loosening up. 'So, you *do* indeed have an alibi. And at what time did you arrive at his house?'

'Well, I left around 11 p.m., so I would have been at Joe's around ten minutes past eleven.'

'And was Anant alive when you left him?'

Mahesh dissolves into a coughing fit. He pours himself some more water and takes a sip. 'Of course, of course, he was alive and well. Why would I kill him?'

'I don't know. You tell me.'

'I didn't kill him, inspector, please.'

'Well, okay, we'll see about that.' Maurya nods slowly and then changes track, 'And what were you guys talking about? You and Anant. You spent a good two hours together.'

'About business, mostly,' Mahesh replies. 'Let me be honest with you: Anant was a damn good fund manager, one of the best. Not the most flexible, but he managed very high returns for long periods of time. When we split up, I lost some of my clients to him. And I wanted to be his ally, not his rival. So, I had gone to his house to ask him to reconsider working together again. There's no ego in our business. The market is supreme, and we've learnt to respect it.'

'And what was his reply?'

'He didn't say yes, but he didn't say no either.'

'Thank you for your time,' Maurya says and rises. 'We'll be in touch.'

FOUR

By the time they are back at the police station, it is late afternoon. Maurya has checked with Mahesh's alibi, Joe, who confirmed the former's presence in his home about ten to fifteen minutes past 11 until 12.30 a.m.

Maurya settles behind his desk and Kiran sits across from him. He barks an order for tea and sandwiches to a young constable. He is exhausted and his stomach is growling.

'They were professional rivals,' suggests Kiran, 'to put it mildly.'

'Yes, that's exactly what I was thinking,' Maurya nods. 'But the way he spoke, he downplayed that so much. Why?'

Kiran shrugs.

Maurya leans forward, his eyes glinting with excitement, 'Check with the neighbours. Hopefully, someone saw Mahesh leave Anant's home at that time. It wasn't that late. Also, check all the CCTV cameras in the surrounding area. As of now, we only have his friend Joe's word of Mahesh leaving that house at 11. Even so, it doesn't make an airtight alibi.' He leans back in his chair and crosses his legs. 'Even if he left the scene of the crime at ten minutes past eleven, as he claims, he could've still killed Anant before leaving the house.'

He looks up at Kiran. 'Have forensics narrowed down the time of death?'

'No,' Kiran shakes her head. 'I don't think that'll be until tomorrow. I'll call them first thing in the morning.'

'Yes, please do. It'll help us.'

He looks up at the television in front of him. 'Increase the volume,' he says to no one in particular.

A recent picture of Anant Kapoor flashes on the screen. 'Some breaking news coming in. This morning, the police discovered the dead body of the famous fund manager Anant Kapoor in his bungalow in Golf Links, Gurgaon. He was thirty-eight and is survived by his thirty-year-old wife, Sanya Kapoor. Our initial sources suggest that it was a murder and the victim was hit by a sharp object. Anant Kapoor was a successful businessman and a regular on various business channels, imparting his wisdom on investing and the merits of financial independence. We had featured him last Diwali in our weekly programme *The Money Show*, and our viewers greatly benefitted from his wisdom. No one has been convicted yet—'

Maurya loses interest and has the television switched off. Investigating the murder of a rich and famous man will not be easy, he thinks, and expels a frustrated sigh. And that too with the victim splashed all over the news! He shakes his head.

The constable places the sandwiches and tea on Maurya's desk. He takes a sip of his tea. Satisfied, he picks up the sandwich and unwraps it. He takes a big, greedy bite off it and chews ravenously. 'Thank you. Very nice,' he says to the constable. Then to Kiran: 'This morning, Vicky told us he returned to the house at 1 a.m., and he seemed certain of this as I asked him twice. How much time do you think it should take to drive from the toll bridge to the house at that time of night?'

'Maximum fifteen minutes,' suggests Kiran. 'If you drive faster, maybe ten.'

'I think so too,' agrees Maurya, his mouth full. 'Check the CCTV cameras at the toll bridge, one of them would've definitely captured his car. I want to know what time he crossed it and entered Gurgaon. As per his statement, it should be around 12.45 a.m. but I won't be surprised if it was sooner, as I have a feeling that he was lying.'

'Sure, makes sense.' She sips her tea.

'I would like to see those fingerprints' result as well.'

'Not before tomorrow, I think.'

Maurya nods slowly. He finishes his sandwich and leans back in his chair, swivelling it sideways, lost in thought. The chair screeches as it moves.

Kiran sips her tea slowly, watching her boss.

Then Maurya stops suddenly, leans forward and asks, 'Did the first team spot any signs of burglary? Do they suspect someone breaking and entering the house with the intention of stealing, or for whatever—'

'No, no,' Kiran replies and shakes her head. 'I checked with the officer who filed the FIR. There was no forced entry. The knobs, latches and locks on all the doors and windows are in perfect shape. It cannot be a case of aggravated robbery.'

'Okay, so it must be one of the three of them, then.'

'Yes, the wife, the brother or the friend.'

'What about the helper? She lives in that house, too.'

Kiran raises an eyebrow. 'You think?'

'Let's find out.'

FIVE

Fifteen minutes later, they're back at 23, Golf Links. This time, there are many cars parked right outside the bungalow and a few of them across the street. Maurya spots a few news channels' cars, some vans, with their fancy satellite dishes mounted on top. There are a lot of news reporters and journalists waiting outside the house, with their microphones and associated paraphernalia.

Maurya and Kiran shoulder past them, but some of the journalists shove their mics in their faces, asking their usual, mundane questions.

'We've got nothing so far,' Maurya spells out his standard reply. 'We're still investigating.'

Kiran rings the doorbell, and the helper, Sharda, opens the door. She recoils at the sight of two police officers.

'I will call madam.'

'No, no,' Maurya says, 'actually we want to talk to you.'

'Me?'

Maurya nods. 'Can we come in?'

Sharda steps aside and they enter. At the far right end of the living room, an old man in saffron robes is reciting a religious mantra in front of about a dozen or so people who are seated in semi-circular rows. Behind him, there is a huge, garlanded portrait of Anant Kapoor.

Sanya, in the front row, looks over her shoulder at the police officers. She begins to rise, but Maurya motions to her to remain seated. The fatso is by her side, he doesn't move.

Maurya and Kiran sit down on the sofa, and Sharda sits nervously on the edge of the chair in front of them.

'When we were here in the morning,' Maurya starts, 'we couldn't speak to you.'

'Relax,' Kiran tells her, as Sharda flushes. 'We just want to talk to you.'

They give her a minute to calm down. Her hands are unsteady and sweat begins to bead her forehead. She purses her lips and nods slowly in agreement.

'Are you okay?' Maurya asks her.

Sharda gives him a nervous nod again.

'Okay, where were you last night between 10 p.m. and 2 a.m.?'

'In . . . in my room.'

'Did you hear anything, a scream or any other unusual sound at this time?'

Sharda shifts her gaze to Kiran and then back to Maurya. 'No, no, nothing.'

'There was a guest in the house around . . .' Maurya consults his diary, 'around 9 p.m. Can you confirm that?'

She looks at the wall clock to her left. 'Yes, should be around that time. Sir and madam had finished their dinner around half past eight. I was doing the dishes when the doorbell rang.'

'And what time did he leave? Did you see him on his way out?'

She shakes her head. 'Sorry, no. I have no idea.'

'And he was a friend?'

'Yes, yes,' she says, nodding. 'Sir was expecting him; he'd told me about his visit during dinner.'

'Had he been to the house earlier?'

'Yes, a few times recently and he was here a few months ago as well.' She grits her teeth and smiles foolishly. 'Sorry, I don't recall when exactly.'

Maurya gives her a casual wave. 'That's fine. And how long have you been working here?'

'Almost two years.'

Maurya steals a quick glance at the other guests in the room. They are all sitting quietly, listening in rapt attention to the priest delivering a monologue on life after death. He stifles a yawn and turns his attention back to Sharda.

'Okay. Did anything unusual happen last night?' he clears his throat. 'I mean anything out of the ordinary . . . anything at all?'

'No, no, sir . . . er . . . actually, not last night, but this morning,' she leans forward and lowers her voice conspiratorially. 'Madam usually steps out of her bedroom after eight, but today she was in the kitchen around seven. I don't think it's a big deal, but I thought I would mention it since you asked.'

'And you never see her that early in the morning?'

She shakes her head, 'No, not usually, no . . . maybe once or, at the most, twice in the past.'

'And did you ask her why?'

'Yes. She said that she didn't sleep well last night.'

Maurya makes a note. 'Okay, that is helpful. Anything else?'

'Actually, one more thing, but I'm not sure if it's unusual.' When she gets an encouraging nod from both the officers, she continues, 'Yesterday, during dinner, sir and madam had a fight.'

Maurya and Kiran exchange a quick glance.

'Go on,' Maurya prompts her.

'I mean, this is nothing unusual because they fight a lot. Sir was always scolding madam; in fact, he would scold his brother as well.'

'Why?'

Here, Sharda lowers her voice further. She casts a quick glance over her shoulder and when satisfied that no one was looking at her, continues in a hushed tone, 'It was always about money. Madam and Vicky are spendthrifts and Anant sir was . . . er . . . I mean he would always lecture them to stop squandering his hard-earned money.'

'And would you know the reason for their argument yesterday?'

'Same, sir,' she says quietly, 'same. Money. What else? I . . . I overheard them from the kitchen. Their anniversary is next month, and madam asked for some . . . something, I . . . I don't know what exactly, but it started from there and sir was very angry.'

'And how was his behaviour towards you?'

'He was nice to me, but sometimes, if I made a mistake, he would scold me a little. He was usually nice.'

'Thank you, Sharda,' Maurya says and gets to his feet. 'You've been very helpful. Very soon we shall know your sir's killer.'

SIX

The next morning, Maurya gets to the station early. He was thinking about the case the night before, and it appears to be straightforward, thus far. The only hitch—there is no witness to the crime.

A lot would depend on the fingerprints they get off that vase. But the killer could have been wearing gloves or he (or she) could have wiped them clean after the crime. Happens all the time. That might make conviction difficult.

Or the fingerprints might not provide a suitable match in the database. What if the killer were a first-time offender? The national database has fingerprints and biometric data of only a few million arrested and convicted persons. The odds are high that they might not get a match at all. More than 80 per cent of the criminals in the country every year are first-time offenders, and Maurya knows it has always been a struggle to identify them.

He shakes his head. If only they could access the Aadhar biometrics data, their lives would be so much easier. However, that decision was taken by the identification authorities a few years ago and access to the Aadhar database was vehemently denied for crime investigations.

He drums on his desk absentmindedly. In his view, the wife is the most likely killer. She doesn't have any alibi; in fact, she admits she was at home. She'd had a fight with her husband just hours before his murder—and there is a witness to that—and to be very frank, he never believed those tears when he first met her. It could have been an accident, he accepts, but his gut tells him that she isn't really devastated by her husband's death.

But why?

Money?

She should get most of her husband's estate if not all, as the brother would certainly bag a handsome share. And the helper mentioned that Sanya likes splurging but was constantly curbed by her husband.

Classic human psychology at play. Avarice. You want something but you can't have it, and then you want it even more. But would she kill her husband for it? Maurya could not answer that with any level of certainty.

There is one more plausible explanation, Maurya thinks. The wife and the brother are complicit. No, they might not be having an affair, as Kiran had postulated, but maybe they both colluded and did it for the money as they couldn't satiate their greed with Anant around. It won't be easy to prove this as both will most probably corroborate the other's version of last night.

Kiran walks through the door and Maurya looks up.

'Ah, there you are!' Maurya perks up. 'What do you have for me?'

She smiles and sits down across from him. 'You don't want to hear this.'

'What now?'

'Forensics managed to get the prints off the vase—nice and dandy, no smears, no smudges, with no signs of interference, surprisingly. In fact, they even managed to capture a palm print, but—'

'But?' Maurya waits patiently.

'They couldn't get a suitable match off their stored files.'

'Fuck, no!' he curses, punching his desk.

'Sorry. What do we do now?'

Maurya knows the drill. It's a high-profile case and his actions are being monitored. If the three suspects do not cooperate, he will have to file the necessary paperwork to get authorization to collect their fingerprints to match them with the extracted prints; it will take some time. He doesn't want to drag on the case for too long.

'And one more thing,' adds Kiran. 'Forensics have narrowed down the time of death. It should be between 11 p.m. to 1 a.m., with low probability of the death occurring in the last half hour. So very likely between 11 p.m. to half past midnight.'

'Good,' says Maurya, slightly relieved. 'That makes it a little easier for us.'

'And I also managed to get the CCTV footage from the toll bridge. You were right. The cameras have Vicky's car—a red Porsche—captured at 12.15. So, he should have been home ideally by 12.30 a.m.'

'And if he drove really fast, 12.25 a.m.?'

'Yes.'

He leans back in his chair. 'So, let's assume he arrived home at 12.25 a.m., went straight down to the basement and killed his brother, five, ten minutes after that and then returned to his room. Possible?'

Kiran nods. 'Possible.'

'Yes, the timelines agree with us. He could have killed Anant at or around 12.30 a.m.'

'And what about the friend, Mahesh?'

Maurya throws out his arms and scowls in frustration. A frown has crept up between his eyes. 'Yeah, well, he could've done it as well. He could've killed Anant before leaving the house, just after eleven, then rushed to his friend's house to be there by 11.10 to avoid suspicion.' He looks at Kiran and, in a sudden, quick gesture, wags a finger at her. 'Hey, did you manage to speak to the neighbours? If he did kill Anant, surely Mahesh would've been in a tearing hurry to reach his friend's house and would've driven the car recklessly.'

'No,' she shakes her head and purses her lips in dismay. 'No witnesses. No one saw him.'

'What about the CCTV cameras?'

'They are far away so we didn't get a clear picture. There were no other suspicious cars or persons around the house either.'

'Shit! Why aren't there any witnesses to this crime?'

It was a rhetorical question and Kiran looks away. They sit quietly for the next few minutes, pondering their next course of action.

The fingerprints.

'Can you at least ask forensics to check the databases from the neighbouring states?' Maurya suggests, but without conviction. 'In fact, from all over the country to see if we get a match—'

'Of course, of course,' Kiran replies. 'They already did that. Standard protocol.'

'Yeah.' Then, with a little more fervour, he adds, 'And through our crime database, you found no record of the three of them for any petty crime, past arrests . . . anything at all?'

'No,' she shakes her head. 'Nothing. They're as clean as a whistle.'

'Which makes me conclude that there had to be a very compelling reason to kill Anant.'

Kiran nods in agreement. 'Why don't we get their fingerprints done? We are well within our rights, aren't we? We don't need a magistrate's permission to fingerprint the accused.'

'Yes, I was thinking that as well,' says Maurya, nodding and running a casual hand through his hair. 'The only caveat is if they refuse, and then things can get a little messy. I want this case to be as smooth as possible. The reporters are watching us like hawks, and I don't want to give them any fodder.'

'What do you propose?'

He mulls over it for a few minutes. 'Let's ask them casually, one by one,' Maurya says finally. 'Tell each one that we know they didn't commit the crime, but we want their fingerprints, as a formality, or just to eliminate them from the prints that we found on the scene of the crime. Disarm them a little. Be nice . . . but not too nice. If they agree willingly, great, get it done; if not, we'll resort to sledgehammer tactics.'

'Okay, sounds good.'

'An innocent person wouldn't mind providing fingerprints as he or she has nothing to hide, but if any one of them hesitates—'

'That'll be our clue as well,' she completes his sentence for him and rises. 'Makes sense. I'll get on it. And while we are at it, you want me to take the helper's prints as well?'

'Yes,' Maurya responds. 'Let's take hers as well.'

'Okay.'

As she turns to leave, Maurya calls out from behind her.

'And make sure you get their palm prints as well.'

SEVEN

Maurya watches Kiran head out the door, and wonders whether she will manage to get the job done without stirring up a ruckus. She is a smart, capable woman who has been working under him for over a year. She has never disappointed him in the past and he hopes that she can pull this off.

Even if he gets the match of one of the accused's fingerprints, he wonders whether that can get the guilty convicted without any objections from the defence counsel in the absence of a witness.

He decides to cross that bridge when he gets to it and heads out for breakfast.

It is a cool and pleasant November afternoon. Kiran finishes her lunch at a small restaurant near the station. She ordered a hearty meal of fried chicken and rice, and she can still taste the sumptuous repast. She has been dieting lately to get back in shape, but she loves to eat and it has been extremely challenging to . . . she's staring at the menu now, specifically the dessert section at the bottom.

She licks her lips and after fighting the voice in her head, puts the menu aside. She signals to the waiter, smiles genially at him and asks for the cheque.

What the heck!

'And get me that chocolate mousse, please,' she calls out.

She deserves it. Earlier in the day, she had managed to convince all the suspects to provide their fingerprints. It went easy.

Too easy, perhaps.

And now she is a little flummoxed. Why did none of them object or, at the very least, hesitate? All of them promptly agreed. Did none of them kill Anant? But how can that be?

The chocolate mousse arrives, and she digs in.

The killer can wait.

The results come in a few minutes before 11 a.m. on Wednesday.

Maurya and Kiran stare at each other in stunned silence. Maurya shakes his head in disbelief. Although he was expecting this, he still finds it hard to fathom.

'So . . .?' Kiran flicks an eyebrow at him from across the desk. 'What are we waiting for? We have an indisputable match. The court cannot possibly reject this evidence.'

'Yes,' he agrees. 'They should not.' He picks up the keys from the desk and rises. 'Let's go.'

They head out the door and get in the jeep. Maurya starts the engine and presses down hard on the accelerator leaving a trail of dust in his wake.

When they arrive at 23, Golf Links, there are more cars and vans, and even more reporters than the last time. The news about the dead fund manager has not stopped streaming on all the news channels. When there is nothing much left to showcase, there are stories of his past, anecdotes from his ex-colleagues and a multitude of interviews of his financial brethren showering praises on his intellect and perseverance.

'Oh, they're going to love this,' Maurya nods towards them as he parks the jeep outside the bungalow.

Once again, he shoves the reporters aside as they head towards the door.

Sanya opens it and the colour drains from her face.

Maurya steps forward. 'Mrs Sanya Kapoor, you are under arrest for the murder of your husband, Anant Kapoor.'

EIGHT

Ten minutes after the police confined Sanya in the holding cell, Vicky is panting at the front door of the station. He looks groggy and dishevelled, like he had just rolled out of bed. His T-shirt is dirty and the pyjamas are crumpled.

He turns his head sideways and, on his right, he spots Maurya sitting behind his desk. He hurries towards him.

'Why have you arrested her?' he demands without preamble. His voice is loud and discordant.

Maurya looks up. Vicky's tone grates on his nerves. 'Lower your fucking voice!'

Vicky huffs irritably. He takes a deep breath and tries to calm himself down. Maurya watches his laborious breathing. He looks as though he has just come in from a jog. A film of perspiration glistens on his forehead.

'Do you have an arrest warrant?' he asks again, the inflection in his voice a few notches down now.

'I don't need an arrest warrant.'

'Why?'

Maurya sighs and wonders whether he should waste precious time explaining a policeman's rights to the nitwit standing in front of him—in the police station, demanding answers from the investigating officer. He has a strong desire to yell at him and throw him out, but he curbs his ire.

'Listen to me carefully,' Maurya says, waggling a cautionary finger at him, trying very hard to control his temper. 'I will say this one time, and one time only. And after that, I want you to be out of here. Are we clear?'

He waits for Vicky to acknowledge this and after a subtle, albeit defiant, nod from him, Maurya continues, 'This is a cognizable offence, and I have reasonable suspicion to believe that your sister-in-law has committed this crime. I am well within my rights to arrest her without a warrant, for proper facilitation of the investigation.'

Maurya pushes his head back, folds his arms across his chest and glares at Vicky, wondering whether he would raise any further objections. Vicky is looking back at him blankly.

'And one more thing,' Maurya adds, 'because I sense you might have this question. This is a non-bailable offence. You are free to hire a defence lawyer for her, but she is not coming out of prison until the trial. After that, it's the court's problem to convict her or . . . well, release her. I doubt the latter, though.'

Even if he has any further questions, Vicky does not ask. He gazes at the inspector stolidly, shakes his head and slowly turns around. After a quick glance around, he walks out the door.

'Fucking idiot!' Maurya says when he is out of earshot.

'What's with his swagger?' Kiran asks, taking a seat, her eyes following him through the door.

'He's a nitwit, what else. Thinks he is some entitled prick.' He shakes his head. 'How's she holding up?'

'She's been sobbing and insisting she didn't kill her husband.'

'Let's talk to her.'

Sanya is escorted out of the holding cell by an old lady constable to a room upstairs. When she enters it, Maurya and Kiran are waiting for her behind a long wooden desk. Sanya takes a deep breath and is relieved that the air here does not smell of mould, betel leaves and urine. The walls of the holding cell in the basement are covered with mildew, and she vomited just few minutes after entering it. Thankfully, there was just one other lady prisoner in her cell, and she had been asleep.

'Thank you,' Maurya tells the constable. 'We'll take it from here.' Then he asks Sanya to take a seat.

Sanya hesitates for a moment, then sits down on a steel chair across from them. It creaks as she settles down. Maurya notes her puffy eyes behind her spectacles. She is looking down at the floor and not making eye contact with them.

Maurya and Kiran exchange a quick glance.

Then Sanya looks up and says softly, 'I didn't kill him, inspector. Please believe me.' She turns to Kiran. 'Why would I kill him? We loved each other. I'm mourning his death and you've—you have . . .' she breaks down.

After giving her a few minutes, Maurya says, 'In full disclosure, we have a camera in this room recording our conversation.'

Sanya sniffles and rubs her nose with the back of her hand.

'We found your fingerprints and your palm prints on the vase, the murder weapon. You don't have an alibi—you were home on the night he was murdered. Your helper told us you'd had a fight with him at dinner. What do you want us to believe?'

'That I didn't kill him!' Sanya yells.

Maurya sits back in his chair. He clicks his tongue and waits.

'Why don't you speak with Mahesh?' Sanya barks, throwing out her arms in outrage. 'He was there with Anant that night, and he hated him! Anant had told me so many times that Mahesh never liked him because Anant was a much better investor. In fact, Mahesh was begging Anant to join him back in his fund. Don't you see?'

Maurya leans forward. 'You could be right,' he says, 'and you will get a fair chance at the trial to prove your innocence before the judiciary. But I have got incriminating evidence against you. As of now, I must hold you and present you before the magistrate.' He pauses as Sanya dabs her eyes. 'I'll be filing my charge sheet and I will need your statement.'

Sanya buries her face in her palms and sobs softly. After a few minutes, she looks up. 'But what is the evidence you have that I killed him? That vase?'

Maurya nods. 'I'm afraid so, yes.'

'But I live in that house! You'll find my fingerprints everywhere!' she protests.

'As I said, you'll get a chance to prove your innocence.'

'But, inspector, please think. If I really killed my husband, wouldn't I erase the fingerprints after the crime or maybe get rid of the murder weapon? How could I be so stupid? How could any killer be so stupid?'

'So why didn't you erase them?'

A snort escapes her nose. 'Because I didn't kill him!' she shakes her head miserably. 'After our fight that day, I went up to my room and booked a flight to Dehradun to visit my mother the following morning.'

'Why?'

'Because I wanted a break! We fought and I wanted a break. What's the big deal in that?'

Maurya is staring at her and listening to every word carefully.

'I woke up early the next day as I had a flight to catch at 10 a.m.,' Sanya continues. Her voice quavers. 'But then, when I went down to the basement to call him for breakfast, he was—he was . . .' Sanya squeezes her eyes shut. She feels the room spin and holds on to the edge of the table.

'Why didn't you tell this earlier, the day we met, that you had booked a flight?' Maurya asks her.

'Because it wasn't relevant!' Sanya says. 'And it wasn't important! How could I know you would have the audacity to arrest me for the murder of my husband?'

Kiran clears her throat. 'Mrs Kapoor, we note your comments but, unfortunately, so far we have to hold you guilty. We request you to cooperate with us and provide your statement.'

'Cooperate with what?' Sanya demands fiercely. 'What do you want me to say?'

'Whatever you think is relevant to the case,' Maurya replies slowly. 'You can start briefly with your background, how you met your husband, your relationship with him, the events of that night and whatever you know about Vicky and your husband's friend, Mahesh. It is important that you try to recall every relevant detail.'

After a long pause, she starts talking.

PART—2

SANYA KAPOOR'S STORY

NINE

I was born into a rich family. My father was a stockbroker who had amassed his wealth in the stock markets. He would tell me that he got rich by a single stroke of luck.

Who was it who had said that a single stroke of genius is far more valuable than a lifetime of uninspired drudgery? Well, I don't recall. But that was the story of my father's life.

When I was young, my father told me that he had shorted the stock market in the Harshad Mehta-led bull run of the early 1990s. He made millions in less than a year. What he did was beyond my understanding. He had explained to me that an investor makes money when the stocks rise in value. But a short-seller (like him) makes money when the stocks go down. In short, they are betting on the company, or the market as a whole, to collapse.

Sounds sadistic, yes, but that is how markets function. There are optimists and then there are pessimists. But my father was an opportunist, and he loved making money.

I was my parents' only child, and my father pampered me a lot. He would buy me whatever I laid my eyes on, no questions asked. I was his precious angel and he was my precious dad.

It is liberating when your money can last you a lifetime. It makes you feel free. Free to do whatever you want, whenever you want and wherever you want. And I was free.

I loved travelling the world, to the remote corners of the planet, hiking, mountaineering, indulging in adventure sports. Life was good. I never worked a single day of my life, although I did complete a degree in law.

No, actually, I did work, but only for few weeks, as an intern at a law firm, but then I quit. Like my father, I hated drudgery. I couldn't be tied to a desk. And, honestly, there wasn't any need for me to work. We had enough money. More than enough.

Little more than two years ago, my father passed away from a stroke. I was shattered. He was my hero. I remember not leaving my bedroom for a month. I was emaciated by the end of it. Parents shouldn't pamper their kids so much that life becomes an ordeal when they're not around.

My mother handled the setback much better than I did. Or, at least, she seemed okay compared to me.

One Sunday afternoon, a few months after my father's death, she came to my room.

'I think you should get married,' she said matter-of-factly.

I looked up from the book that I was reading. 'Where did that come from?'

'Sanu, you're approaching thirty now.'

'Is that your answer?'

She sighed and sat down beside me. 'I'm talking about Anant. I met his father yesterday. Your father and he were great friends. And you know Anant, don't you? You've met him a few times in the past.'

'But isn't he married?'

'He *was* married. His wife died last year in a car accident.'

I put a hand to my heart. 'Oh God!' But then I was puzzled. 'You want me to marry a widower?'

'So what? He's single again and they're family friends.' Then she narrowed her eyes at me. 'Do you have anybody else in mind?'

I put the book aside. 'No, I don't, and I'm not even interested. I like my freedom, Mom!' I shook my head in mild exasperation. 'Marriage will constrain me. Most guys are like that, chauvinists, wanting to control the lives of their wives. Besides, Dad has left us so much money. Anyone who wants to marry me will be a gold-digger.'

'Not Anant,' she replied, shaking her head. 'He's doing very well for himself.' She rose in disappointment. 'Can you at least consider it? He's a good man from a good family and he's interested in you.'

And so, I ended up meeting him casually. My mother was right. He was a good man, respectful, warm and funny. We went out on a few dates, watched movies together, went on long drives outside Delhi. I liked talking to him, listening to him. He was grounded, despite his success.

In those days, he was running a fund management company with his old colleague Mahesh Murthy—a company they had started a year ago. I always thought Mahesh was envious of Anant. He was five years senior to Anant, but not as popular or as successful as Anant was. Anant told me later that he had wanted to start a company independently, but Mahesh had begged and pleaded with him to take him on as a partner. Anant regretted it after a while, sold his share to Mahesh and ventured out on his own a year later.

I was never an investor or a saver, and I never understood his business. Once, he did try explaining his investment process. It went over my head. Financial mumbo-jumbo, I had replied, and told him that I knew how to spend money, earning it wasn't really my forte. We had laughed over it.

I could see he was doing well. He was a regular on the financial news channels and his interviews featured in some of the most prominent newspapers. He was one of the youngest fund managers in the country who ran his own fund.

That winter, we went on a road trip to Jaipur. We had dinner at a fancy restaurant, and after our meal, he proposed to me. I told him that I needed to think about it.

I wasn't hung up on the fact that he was a widower, that was fine; my concern was that I wasn't even sure that I ever wanted to tie the knot. With anyone. But, after a lot of goading from my mother and emotional blackmail, I gave in.

The week after he proposed, I telephoned him at his office and accepted his proposal.

We got married two months later, in December.

Everything was great in our marriage, although I must admit, just as every other couple, we had our share of arguments and disagreements. And surprisingly, they were always about money, a commodity which we had in abundance. We had a completely opposite worldview on money—180 degrees apart.

I admit that I've always been a spendthrift; I have never even, till date, looked at the price tag of what I buy. I was brought up that way, my father never questioned me about it.

But Anant, well, he was a hoarder, extremely cautious with his money. He wouldn't spend an extra dime unless he really had to. And I respected that. He told me that he had worked very hard for his money and he did not want us to fritter it away.

His brother, Vicky, isn't like him at all. In fact, he is like me. Actually, he's worse. Like me, he hasn't worked his entire life, but he was dependent on his big brother, ten years his senior. Unfortunately, Vicky is addicted to gambling and that makes matters worse.

Vicky has a giant television screen across the bed in his room. All day long he is sprawled in front of it, his phone in hand, barking betting orders. He bets on cricket matches mostly, but sometimes on other sports as well. During cricket tournaments, you'll never find him outside his room; he locks himself in.

Anant discussed this a few times with me. His brother's lifestyle saddened him a lot. He castigated Vicky a zillion times in front of me, in front of strangers, almost humiliating him, but Vicky didn't budge. He urged Vicky umpteen times to quit gambling and to join his firm, but to no avail.

Recently, Vicky got himself in a soup. He owes a bookie about two crore rupees on a bet he lost. He didn't have the nerve to tell Anant about it, let alone ask him for the money. He had shared his predicament with me, hoping that I would help him.

But what could I have done? I told him to speak to Anant and not keep any secrets from him. After a lot of thought, I think he did speak to him eventually, but I'm not sure about the outcome. Anant would have been incensed, I'm fairly sure of that.

Between Anant and I, we had carefully built a cordial demarcation. I wouldn't squander his money and bought all the luxuries that I am so used to with my father's money, even my cars. It went well for a few months. But

I think this anguished him a little, although he didn't mention it.

Then last month, he told me that he earned enough for both of us, and that I should avoid making this distinction between our wealth. I thought I hurt his male ego and tried to balance it as best as I could.

That night, we were discussing our anniversary plans for next month. I wanted to go on a world cruise but he complained that he was very busy, that December was a very important month for markets and his presence in the country was crucial.

What happened next was my mistake, and I accept it. But it wasn't intentional. I might have said it spitefully that I could sponsor the cruise—it angered him; and what started as a small disagreement ended up turning into a full-blown argument.

After dinner, I went up to my room, booked my flight tickets to spend a few days with my mother in Dehradun and take a break from my overbearing husband. Isn't this normal? All married couples bicker from time to time. You put any two individuals together for a long period of time and they will inevitably and invariably fall out over something eventually. But would you kill your spouse over a disagreement?

The next morning, I found him dead when I went into his study to summon him for breakfast.

TEN

Back at his desk, Maurya sits still and feels a sense of foreboding. *What if she's telling the truth?* There would be a ruckus and the media would eat him for breakfast. Maybe he had arrested her too early. But that was because he has never been a fan of cases involving famous people. It was always better to file your charge sheet as early as you could and hand over the matter to the court. The other, run-of-the-mill cases, involving commoners, didn't elicit any spotlight and one could go about investigating them at one's own pace.

Kiran walks over to him. 'What's up, boss?'

Maurya hesitates. 'I . . . I was just thinking that maybe we arrested her too early.'

Kiran sits down. 'You're thinking that Mahesh could have it done as well, right? What with all the professional rivalry between them.'

'And the brother, too.' Maurya sits up in his chair. 'I mean, look, he wanted that money—two crores! His brother wouldn't have just handed it over to him. It's not a small amount.'

'And so, he did it—'

'He could have.'

'Yeah, he could,' she nods slowly. After a few moments of silence, she suggests, 'So let's go talk to him.'

'Yes, but let's talk to Mahesh first. And then we see the brother.'

Twenty minutes later they are sitting in Mahesh's office, escorted by the young receptionist. Mahesh is on the phone, sitting across the desk. He replaces the receiver after a minute and turns to his guests with an affable smile.

'I'm very sorry,' he looks down at the telephone, 'that was a very important client and I had to finish the conversation.'

'No, no, that's fine,' Maurya replies, waving a hand. He looks over his shoulder at the television playing financial news. Stock quotes of various companies are ticker-taping across at the bottom of the screen.

'Let me put the TV on mute.' He reaches for the remote on his desk and presses a button. 'Right. What can I do for you, sir? I hear you've already arrested Mrs Kapoor.'

'Yes, we have, but we still have some questions left.'

'Sure. I'll answer them as best as I can.'

Maurya leans back in the chair and takes a moment to ask his first question. 'How well do you know Mrs Kapoor?'

'Only . . . casually,' Mahesh replies. 'I've never really had a lot of interaction with her.'

'And how would you describe the relationship with her husband?'

Mahesh frowns. 'I . . . I don't know. I mean, Anant never talked much about her. You see, he was a very private man.'

'I understand,' Maurya says. 'But when you were around them, what was the attitude of Anant towards his wife?'

'Normal. I think they were very much in love.'

'Did you ever see them quarrelling or was he ever disrespectful to his wife?'

'No, no,' Mahesh shakes his head. 'But, like I said, I wasn't around her a lot.' He pauses. 'Actually once, last year, at their anniversary, I did witness them having an argument. I was at a distance, so I don't know the reason, but Anant was—well, what appeared to me from that distance—yelling at her, and then she walked away. But you see Anant was short-tempered. I mean he was a good guy, but when he got angry, he had an outburst he couldn't control. He had to let out all the steam from within. And he would yell at a lot of people, even in our office. He was a Scorpio and what do you expect from a Scorpio?'

'Okay. Anything else you recall?'

'No. Like I said they were a nice couple, pretty much in love with each other. And he rarely talked about her, although he did talk a lot about his brother, Vicky.'

Maurya's curiosity is piqued. 'What did he talk about?'

Beside him, Kiran is peering at Mahesh with renewed interest.

'His brother was . . . well, he had some vices. I . . . I don't know, but the brothers were poles apart. Anant was so dignified and organized, focused on his work, and Vicky was—well, he was extremely lazy and laidback, never worked a day in his entire life. He gambled his brother's money and sometimes . . . no, most of the time, lost it. And Anant would be miffed at him and tell me later that he just couldn't fix his brother.'

'But why did Anant give his brother money for gambling?'

'He didn't.' Mahesh shakes his head. 'I mean, not wilfully. Vicky would pester him and emotionally blackmail him, and what not. See, he is twenty-eight years old, about ten years younger to Anant, so Anant did feel some sort of responsibility, that of an older brother, towards him. And then there was this whole confusion about sharing their father's money.'

'What about it?' Maurya asks impatiently.

'See, when their father died, there was no will, so the brothers had decided amicably to split the money that he left them. Then three years ago, when we were starting our company, Anant needed capital, so he put in his brother's share as well, promising Vicky that he would be able to grow his money by investing it in the stock markets. Whenever Vicky asked for money, Anant couldn't refuse, but he didn't withdraw the money from the fund. He gave him money from the commissions that we were earning. I don't know when it got out of hand, but Vicky's gambling really took off, his bets became very big and he was consistently losing money. Anant had to sell some of the units in the fund to arrange that cash, sometimes it was in crores—that was the size of his bets! Anant told me that not only had Vicky managed to lose all the money of his father's share, but he had lost some of Anant's money as well. And then the disharmony between the brothers began; they stopped getting along with each other. Earlier, they were the quintessential loving brothers that every Indian mother desires. That completely changed. Anant would reprimand him very often and tell him off, sometimes even in front of me, but Vicky hasn't changed a bit.'

'And when did this start, I mean the disharmony between the brothers?'

Mahesh sits back in his chair and mulls over it for a moment or two. 'I'm not very sure, but I think it was sometime last year.'

'Okay.' Maurya pulls out his diary and makes a note. 'And about the company that you and Anant founded together, you told me earlier that it was,' he flips a few pages of the diary 'it was started three years ago, and then Anant quit and started his own company about a year ago. Correct?'

Mahesh nods.

'Whose idea was it to start the company together?'

Mahesh shrugs. 'Both of us.'

'And are you sure about that?'

'Why—why do you ask me that? How does it matter?'

'Please just answer the question.'

Mahesh looks at him, puzzled. 'Yes . . . yes, I'm sure of that.'

'Then why did he quit if it had been a unanimous decision to start a company together?'

Kiran notices Mahesh's body tense at the question. The calm demeanour has transmogrified to that of a defenceless prey when it is cornered by its predator. He pulls out a handkerchief and dabs at his forehead.

'But I . . . I already told you that last time, inspector.'

'I want to hear it again,' Maurya insists. 'Tell me again.'

'Well, he . . . he and I were very different investors. We had different strategies, and it was getting difficult to reach an agreement on . . . you know, what to buy, when to buy, when to sell, and . . . and so on.'

'Okay,' Maurya says coldly. 'And then why did you want him back with you?'

'I think . . . I . . . I told you this last time as well.'

'Again.'

'Yeah, so he was very good at what he did, and—and when we split, I . . .' he pauses to catch his breath, 'I lost some of my clients to him. I wanted us to be in the same team.'

'Were you jealous of him?'

'No, no, of course not!' Mahesh protests with a vehement shake of his head. 'He was a friend. I've known him for about ten years.'

'Yes, I agree,' Maurya says approvingly and nods, 'but he was your junior, and he was doing better than you. Surely you would have felt a pang of jealousy?'

Mahesh stares askance at the man who has the nerve to accuse him in his own office and wonders how to reply to that question. He thinks of taking a different approach. 'I don't understand the context of the question. You have already arrested Mrs Kapoor for Anant's murder. Do you want to arrest me as well? Should I call a lawyer?'

Maurya turns to Kiran for a brief glance, then back at Mahesh. He waves at him casually, 'I'm not arresting you. This is a simple Q & A.' He takes a deep breath. 'Okay, never mind. Just one last question, I promise, and then we leave you.'

Mahesh's jaw drops. 'Yes?'

'You mentioned that you were meeting Anant that night to request him to collaborate again. So that was your first time making that request to him, right? I mean after you had split.'

Mahesh swallows hard. 'Yes, yes, that . . . that was the night I asked him for the first time.'

'And you mentioned that he said,' he refers to his diary again, 'and I quote here: "He didn't say yes, but he didn't say no." Is that correct?'

'Yes.'

Maurya stares at him for a long time. 'Okay, thank you. I have nothing else to ask.' He rises and then adds, 'For now.'

As he steps out of his office with Kiran in tow, he wonders why Mahesh continues to lie.

ELEVEN

They proceed towards Anant's bungalow after a quick lunch at a south Indian restaurant near Mahesh's office. At 3 p.m., it was empty, and the food arrived on their table in a jiffy. They gobbled it up fast. Maurya wanted to speak to Vicky as quickly as possible and decide his next course of action. He has been feeling uneasy at the thought of keeping Sanya behind bars when she could be innocent.

As he is driving, he turns to face Kiran, 'Listen, I want you to get me the phone records of the victim and the three suspects, say for the last two to three months.' He looks ahead and turns off from the highway. 'Look out for any anomalies, anything odd, anything that catches your eye and report back.'

'Sure,' she says. 'I'll get on it.'

'And Sanya said she had booked a flight to Dehradun the night before the murder. Check her credit card statement and the flight details. I want to know the timing of the flight and when she made the booking.'

'Okay.'

'Also, for Anant and Mahesh's companies, get me the financial documents, their profit and loss statements, tax records and any other relevant documents. Let's see how they've been doing. We'll speak to a financial consultant if required.'

'Okay.' She pulls out her phone. 'Let me make a few calls.'

As she starts talking on her phone, Maurya feels discomfort in the pit of his stomach. *It could have been Mahesh as well. Damn! Why didn't I see this earlier?* He grits his teeth and makes a sharp left turn.

They arrive a few minutes later, and Maurya walks hurriedly to the door. Kiran trails after him, still on the phone.

The helper, Sharda, opens the door. She looks tired and bewildered at the sight of Maurya.

'Is Vicky home?'

'Yes.'

He steps inside. 'Please call him.'

Sharda nods and turns around. After a casual glance around the living room, Maurya sits down on the sofa. Kiran joins him.

After ten minutes Vicky ambles towards them, his hands inside the pockets of his trousers. If he is surprised to see them, he doesn't show it.

'Yes?'

Maurya glances at his wristwatch. 'It took you ten minutes to come here from your room?'

'Yes, I was busy.'

'Which team have you bet on?'

At first, Vicky doesn't understand the question. When it registers, the floor beneath him seems to shift. The colour drains from his face, and he gapes in dismay at the inspector.

'I'm assuming you do know that betting is illegal in the country, and I can charge you for it.' When Vicky doesn't answer, Maurya motions him to sit down. Vicky approaches him apprehensively and sits on a chair across from him.

'It's your lucky day today,' Maurya flashes a noncommittal smile. 'I won't charge you for gambling and you can keep losing your money. I want to ask about your brother and sister-in-law.'

Vicky makes no comment, but he feels a prickly sensation on the back of his neck.

'But first, I want to know why you lied to me.'

'L . . . lie . . .?'

'Yes.' Maurya nods. 'You see, you told me that on the night of your brother's murder, you were home at 1 a.m. But you were at the toll bridge fifteen minutes past midnight. Why did it take you forty-five minutes to get back here? It is less than 10 kilometres. Did you go somewhere else?'

Vicky shakes his head. 'No, no, I didn't go anywhere else.'

'Then it shouldn't have taken you more than fifteen minutes to arrive here. So how come?'

Vicky tries to remember. He shouldn't have been driving in the first place as he was drunk that night. He doesn't want to mention it now.

Maurya is watching him, waiting for an answer. 'Vicky?'

'What? Yeah, sorry. I . . . I could've been here early, I don't remember exactly. It could have been a few minutes before one. I . . . I didn't check the time.'

Maurya leans back and eyes him more closely. 'I don't think I can believe you. You sounded pretty certain last time that you were here at 1 a.m.'

'It was a mistake. I . . . I could've been here at 12.40 or 12.45. Like I told you last time, I went straight to bed.'

'Okay, fair enough,' Maurya says. 'I can give you the benefit of doubt, but the problem I have is that your brother was killed between 11 p.m. and 1 a.m., so your timing in the house is important to the case.'

'But you already arrested my—'

'Yes, I know. But you could have been complicit in the murder as well.'

Kiran casts a sidelong glance at her boss, startled by the direct accusation. It is almost as if he made a casual comment about the weather. But Maurya is a straight shooter, and she admires that about him.

Vicky is taken aback by the statement. He has lost his bearings like a ship out at sea without its compass. Then he leans forward. 'Sorry, what did you say?'

'You heard me.'

'No, why would I kill my brother?'

'Because you wanted two crore rupees.'

Vicky finds it difficult to breathe now. He digs his nails into the meat of his palms and tries to act normal. If they know this, what else do they know?

'Yes, yes, that I agree, but I didn't kill my brother,' he says, nodding like an obedient schoolboy. 'I did need the money. I made a horrible bet and lost.'

'Okay. I'm glad that you're being honest. And did your brother give you the money?'

He hesitates before answering, 'No, he didn't.'

'Why?'

Vicky looks at the floor and takes a deep breath. He considers the question. Why did his brother not give him the money? Fine, he hadn't acted responsibly on his part lately. That he couldn't deny. But this time he really needed it. How could his brother refuse?

He looks up. 'I . . . I don't know. He was—well, he didn't like the gambling and—'

'Before you answer that,' Maurya cuts in sharply, stretching out his arm, 'perhaps you can tell us why you needed that much money?'

'I lost a bet on a cricket match, and I had to return that money. The bookie, um, he . . . he is threatening me,' Vicky runs a shaky hand through his hair, 'and, I . . . I mean he is a dangerous guy. I shouldn't have messed with him. I told this to my brother and promised him that I would stop betting, but I had to settle this last score. I don't know why, but he point-blank refused me and told me that he'd rather give his money to charity than give it to me. I was shocked at my brother's nonchalance; I mean, he was a very loving and caring brother, but then he just threw me to the wolves.'

'And then?'

'And then nothing. I still owe the money.'

'And who is this bookie?'

'I don't know,' Vicky replies and sighs in exasperation. 'He runs a very discreet operation. I don't know his name or even his whereabouts. We pass our orders through intermediaries. But I do know that he is a big shot and—'

'I don't care,' Maurya interjects again. 'Tell me more about your brother. You say he had been a very loving brother, then why the sudden change of heart?'

There is a long silence.

'Although,' Maurya adds as an afterthought, 'with a brother like you, I'm not surprised.'

Vicky rolls his eyes and says, 'I already told you that I accept my mistake. And I told Anant that I would change, but he obviously . . .' he stops to organize his thoughts, 'well . . . he was fed up with it and I don't think he believed me. Yes, he was a very good brother and I admit I screwed up, mostly due to my betting. I lost a lot of money, some of his as well, and so . . . so because of that he must have changed and despised me towards the end of his life. We were not really on talking terms for the past few months.' He stops talking and lowers his head. After a few moments of silence, he utters in a quavering voice, 'And I feel terrible about that.'

Maurya gives him a moment, then asks, 'And what about you? What did you think of your brother right before he died?'

'I was angry with him for not giving me the money,' he replies softly.

Maurya makes a show of cleaning his ears. 'Sorry, what did you say?'

Vicky looks up. 'I . . . I was very annoyed with him. He had so much money and he didn't want to share it with me.'

'And what about Sanya?'

'Why would she care? She has enough of her own.'

'Yes, but how was their relationship?'

'It was fine.'

'Did they fight?'

Vicky's forehead wrinkles in confusion. 'Yeah, I guess.'

Maurya shifts closer to him. 'Can you be more specific, please?'

Vicky takes a moment to answer. 'They would argue, I mean, like any other couple. My brother wasn't very easy to get along with. I mean he was nice and all, but occasionally he would lose it, and he would demean others, you know act a little haughty and say things like, "I've achieved so much in life, what have you done?" or "You dumbo! you know nothing!" I would bear most of the brunt of his anger, of course, but sometimes it would be Sanya as well.'

'And what do you think of Sanya?'

'She is very nice,' he replies. 'I like her. We . . . we get along well with each other. But it is extremely shocking that you've arrested her. Why would she kill her husband?'

Yes, Maurya wanted to tell him, *maybe she didn't kill him. Maybe you did. Or perhaps you did it together.*

'That's what we're trying to find out,' Maurya answers absently and gets to his feet. He stands motionless as if he has forgotten something. Then he turns to Vicky and asks, 'Hey, how are you going to return the money to that bookie?'

Vicky shrugs.

Maurya smiles. 'Let me know if you find out more about that bookie.'

Vicky nods slowly in response and watches them head out the door, heaving a sigh of relief.

TWELVE

At the door, just as he is about to step out, Maurya stops. He turns around on his heels and Kiran looks at him in surprise.

'Hey, Vicky,' Maurya raises his voice from the door, 'do you mind taking us down to your brother's room?'

'Sure.'

Vicky leads Maurya and Kiran down to the basement, towards his brother's study. The door is open, and they step in.

Behind the huge desk, there is a wooden cabinet that houses hundreds of books. To the right, there is another wooden cabinet, about knee-high, running the entire breadth of the room and stops a few inches before the entrance door. There are a few showpieces on top of it, and Maurya guesses the killer would have likely picked the vase from here. He spots a few awards as well, towards the end of the cabinet. He steps closer. *He was an accomplished guy indeed*, Maurya thinks. Anant had won the best fund manager award for three consecutive years, another award for the youngest fund manager and yet another for the best entrepreneur in the financial industry. There are a few more that Maurya does not bother reading.

'What's that?' he points to a door behind the leather chair.

'Door,' says Vicky flatly.

'Yeah, sorry, I meant, where does it lead to?'

'Outside.'

Maurya wonders how he had missed it the first time. He walks towards it, reaches for the knob and pushes the door open. There is a tiny, walled garden and a white-marbled walkway snaking past it that leads to a sheltered staircase on the other side.

'Oh!' he snorts. He looks over his shoulder, 'And where do those lead to?'

'Upstairs, to the back of the house.'

'So, there is another entrance to the house?'

Vicky nods. 'Yes. From the back. Sometimes Anant would park his car at the back and enter the house from here.'

'Hmm. Okay.'

They walk towards the spiral staircase, Maurya leading them, and they walk up the stairs. Once upstairs, Maurya finds an automated iron gate to the right. To his left, there is a small muddy patch on the otherwise green back yard. Maurya bends down and examines it closely.

'Look,' he points out.

Kiran sits on her haunches. 'There are two pairs of footprints.'

'Yes, and they look fresh, don't they?'

Kiran nods.

Maurya looks over his shoulder at Vicky. 'Did you ever enter from here?'

'Yeah, just once, last year.'

Maurya tuts. 'And Sanya wouldn't really be entering from here and take the longer route to the living room.' He considers it. *'Mahesh?'* He pulls out his phone and clicks a few pictures.

He rises. 'Don't erase these,' he tells Vicky. 'Let's go,' he says to Kiran.

By the time they are back at the station, it is close to 5 p.m. Maurya gets behind his desk and rubs his tired face. He is not feeling too well. The case is not going very smoothly and now he is sure that he has arrested Sanya prematurely. Not that he does not suspect her; she remains a prime suspect due to the evidence, but now he has reason to believe that the other two suspects could have very likely been involved. But the problem is that Sanya is behind bars and the other two are not, and how does he correct this mistake?

Fifteen minutes later, Kiran walks over to his desk. 'I have the telephone records,' she says, putting the papers on his desk and a cup of coffee.

'Thanks,' Maurya says, picking up the coffee and briefly glancing at the papers. 'What did you find? I have a headache.' He takes a sip.

'I found a few interesting things, but they complicate the case further.'

Maurya leans forward, a little more alert now. 'Go on.'

'On the night of the murder, there was a call on Anant's cell phone. At 10.55 p.m. That was minutes before the murder. The call lasted for about ten minutes. The caller was Vicky.'

'Hmm. Interesting. What else?'

Kiran starts grinning. 'And you'll love me for guessing this; I only wish I had bet you on it.'

'What?'

'I had guessed on the very first day that Vicky and Sanya might be having an affair,' she brags and raises a triumphant eyebrow. 'And you pooh-poohed my theory. Well, get this: in the last three months, there were sixty-eight calls between them—some of them lasting more than an hour!'

Maurya's jaw drops, and he puts the coffee cup back on the desk. He reaches for the papers and pores through them in bewilderment. He puts them back on the desk and looks up. 'Really?'

Kiran cocks her head in delight, 'I told you so.'

'So, my earlier intuition that they might have done it together might be—' he stops. 'What else do you have?'

Kiran grimaces. 'This part complicates it. I thought that it had to be either the brother or the wife, or both of them together, but this—' she pauses and takes a sip of her coffee. 'Mahesh had called Anant eighteen times in the last three months, and how many times did Anant call him back? . . . Zero!'

'Oh God!' he exclaims with a shake of his head. 'And how long did they speak for?'

'Only for a few minutes each time. In some cases, less than a minute. It looks like Anant just hung up on him.'

'So that means Anant wasn't really interested in talking to Mahesh and he has been lying. He was badgering Anant to get back together, calling him repeatedly, and Anant was clearly declining the offer.'

'That is likely the case,' Kiran replies. 'And Mahesh also said that the night of the murder was the first time he had asked Anant to get back together.'

'That was a lie too. I could read his face and get that he was lying.'

Maurya sits back in his chair and interlocks his hands behind his head. Kiran sips her coffee and peers at him, a coy smile on her lips.

That is a solid motive, Maurya thinks, that of professional rivalry. If Anant was a very strong competitor, either get him on your side or eliminate him.

'Hey what about the financial documents? Did you get them?'

'Yes,' she nods. 'I did and went through them rather briefly. A lot went above my head, but I did get the gist of it. The AUM,' she looks down at the paper, 'assets under management, basically the total money that the funds have for investment, had been going down steadily in the past year for Mahesh's company. And no guesses as to where that money was going.'

'Fuck, no!' Maurya grunts. 'It all adds up. Mahesh indeed had a solid motive to kill him.' He exhales a long sigh and whistles.

'And what about those footprints?'

He ponders over it for a few moments. 'See, here's how I think it could have played out. Mahesh visits Anant, begging him to get back together. Anant refuses. Mahesh exits through the front door and by the time he gets to his car, he is fuming. But he doesn't want to enter through the front door again to avoid the helper seeing him again. So, he calls Anant for . . . I don't know, he must have made something up, and Anant opens the back door, and Mahesh heads back down again.' He leans forward. 'And this time he kills Anant.'

'Are you sure?'

He waves a hand. 'Of course not.' He considers those footprints again. 'The problem with the footprints is that they don't prove anything. How do we know they are from Mahesh's shoes? We don't. They could belong to anybody. Nobody saw him enter through the back door. There are no cameras. The court will simply not accept it.'

'So, they're useless?'

Maurya's lips curve in a crooked smile. 'Not if we were to do some fishing.' He picks up the phone and consults the number from his diary. He dials and waits.

'Hello.'

'Hi, Mr Murthy, this is inspector Maurya.'

There is silence at the other end. Then a curt acknowledgement.

'We know that on the night of the murder, you entered the house again, this time through the back door, around five minutes past eleven. A neighbour saw you and we have your footprints. I need to interrogate you further and I want you at the police station.'

Maurya looks up at Kiran and listens in rapt attention.

'Yes, tomorrow morning is fine,' he says and hangs up.

'What did he say?'

'That he did go back to the house through the back door.'

THIRTEEN

Kiran's mouth is wide open. She is sure that she didn't hear Maurya correctly. She leans forward and asks in a raspy voice, 'What?'

'Yes,' Maurya confirms slowly. 'He admits it.'

They take a minute to soak in the new information.

After a few minutes of silence, Maurya says, 'Even if he did go down, that does not mean he killed Anant, although I'm very curious to know why he went down again and why did he not tell us this the last two times we met him . . .' he trails off and drums his knuckles on the desk. His forehead wrinkles in confusion. 'There are three possible scenarios the way I see it now, and I'm kicking myself for not thinking of them earlier. The first is that Mahesh killed Anant—he had a motive and he hid his second entry into the house through the back door. The second possibility is that Sanya and Vicky collaborated and killed him, maybe because of the money, but Sanya could have had some other reason, or maybe because they were having an affair. And the third—' he pauses and releases a shaky breath, 'well, I'm not sure . . . I mean this sounds far-fetched, but I've been thinking that the three of them might have colluded and killed Anant.'

'But—but . . . why?'

'Because it's all so confusing or maybe they've purposely made it confusing for us. Mahesh and Vicky had motives, but the evidence is stacked against Sanya. Can this be coincidental? Extremely unlikely, if you ask me. The three suspects knew each other. Maybe they planned it this way. If we don't have irrefutable evidence against any one of them—'

'We cannot convict them,' Kiran completes for him.

'Yes, exactly. Or . . . or . . . maybe the evidence was planted against Sanya, and Mahesh or Vicky killed Anant.' He shakes his head. 'I'm not sure. It could be either of the possibilities. I have not managed to eliminate any of them.'

'But we have Sanya behind the bars now.'

'Yes, that's the problem.' He thumps his fist on the desk. 'You know, I was thinking about what Sanya told us in the morning. That she couldn't have been so stupid as to leave her fingerprints behind if she had indeed killed him. And, you know what, I agree with her. Although she isn't the smartest woman around, what with all that squandering of her father and husband's money her entire life, she cannot be so dumb either as to leave such incriminating evidence behind.'

'Or maybe she *is* that dumb?'

'But she also said that she studied law,' Maurya counters. 'I mean, she never really practised it, but she cannot be so dumb as to not know to conceal evidence after committing a crime. Or maybe she killed him, panicked and ran away.' He shakes his head. 'But where? To her room? She also had a flight to catch, remember?'

'Yes, I did check it out. She booked her ticket at half past nine that night for a morning flight at 10 a.m. So that kind of tallies with what she told us.'

'There we go,' Maurya flings out his arms in despair. 'So, she books her flight, goes down and kills her husband, then comes back to her room, sleeps and wakes up early in the morning—which is not her usual time—to catch the flight. She has to be the world's most cold-blooded killer or a completely air-headed bimbo if she killed him.'

'It doesn't make any sense.'

'It doesn't, right?'

Kiran does not reply and watches Maurya scowl in annoyance. What had appeared to be an open-and-shut case in the beginning has suddenly turned on its head.

But there is still that elephant in the room and Kiran points it out, 'So, what do you propose we . . . er . . . we should do with Sanya?'

'We have to release her.'

FOURTEEN

At around six that evening, Sanya is escorted back to the interrogation room and once again she is relieved to be there, out of that stinking dump of a holding cell. When she steps in, Maurya and Kiran are sitting behind the desk. She steps forward and takes a seat across from them.

'Hello, Mrs Kapoor,' Maurya starts off with a genial smile.

Sanya nods.

Maurya clears his throat. 'The circumstances of our visit now are different from this morning.' He shuffles through some papers in front of him. 'To cut a long story short, we will be releasing you because the evidence we have against you is insufficient.'

'That's because I didn't kill him,' replies Sanya, returning Maurya's smile. Kiran notices that the colour has come back to her cheeks, and she suddenly appears buoyant.

'Well, let me be explicitly clear on that,' says Maurya. 'Although we're releasing you, you are still a suspect. We believe you could have killed your husband either in isolation or . . . through collusion.'

'What?'

Maurya picks up a paper. 'These are the telephone records of you and your brother-in-law. Would you kindly explain why there were sixty-eight telephone calls between the two of you in the last three months when you live in the same house?'

Sanya's heart begins to pound. She swallows and tries to keep a calm exterior. 'I . . . I . . . I did tell you this morning that . . . er . . . Vicky had a gambling addiction and recently a bookie has been harassing him to return his two crores. We . . . we would talk about it mostly and I would urge him to quit. Anant, after all, despised Vicky for that.'

Maurya is not convinced. He leans back in his chair and crosses his arms across his chest. He watches Sanya closely with a tilt of his head. 'Mrs Kapoor, are you telling me that you spoke to him for more than an hour in some instances about his gambling addiction?'

Sanya's lips quiver. 'Y . . . yes . . . yes . . .' she stammers.

Maurya narrows his eyes at her and continues glaring. He turns for a quick glance at Kiran and nods stealthily.

'Mrs Kapoor,' says Kiran, 'are you having an affair with your brother-in-law?'

Sanya scrunches up her face. 'What? No!'

'Are you sure?'

'Well, y . . . yes.'

'We can't prove that now,' Maurya says, 'can we?'

'There's nothing to prove,' Sanya says firmly.

Maurya wonders whether he should believe her. For now, he does not have a choice. He has thought this through thoroughly. He realizes that he does not have sufficient evidence against her, and he does not want to commit a second, and graver, mistake in continuing to hold her to cover his first mistake. He picks up a paper from the sheaf and places it in front of Sanya.

'These are you release papers,' he says. 'Please sign them.' He hands her a pen. 'You also need to sign an undertaking to appear, as and when required, before the magistrate empowered to take cognizance of this case.'

Sanya gives the papers a cursory glance and signs them without hesitation. She gets to her feet. 'May I leave?' she asks.

'Yes.' Maurya nods. As she gets to the door, Maurya says, 'Mrs Kapoor, I'll be watching you. Like I said earlier, you're still a suspect.'

Sanya stops at the door, a little edgy.

'And I'm still not convinced by your answer that you spoke to Vicky for hours about his gambling addiction.'

Sanya turns and takes a step forward. 'Yes, I did. But we also discussed his estranged relationship with his brother. I wanted them to bond again like old times. We did speak about that bookie, that he shouldn't get in trouble with dangerous people like that. My brother-in-law is very naïve, and I just wanted to make sure that he was safe.'

As she walks out the door, Maurya has an unsettling feeling that she is hiding something.

FIFTEEN

The next morning, the first thing Maurya decides to do at the station is answer the questions of a swarm of journalists waiting for him. He has been expecting this and had rehearsed the answer while having his breakfast at home.

He steps out wearing his sunglasses, Kiran beside him. The sun is out, and the day is crisp and clear. At the sight of him, a hushed silence falls on the group. The reporters are looking expectantly at him.

One of them demands, 'Why did you arrest Mrs Sanya Kapoor, only to release her the same day, when the police were not certain if she committed the crime?'

A few more questions are fired at him. Maurya raises his right arm.

'It is correct that we arrested Mrs Kapoor prematurely, but we had a valid reason. Actually, we had two. First, we wanted to restrain her from making any inducement to any person acquainted with the facts of the case. Second, we wanted to avoid the tampering of evidence in any manner. However, we had to release her as, after our investigation, we had insufficient evidence against her.'

'But sir, surely the evidence—'

'Please rest assured that police are doing their job efficiently and very soon we will be putting the culprit behind bars. No more questions, please.'

He turns around amid the uproar behind him and steps back into the station.

'That was quick,' says Kiran, smiling, 'and smart. At least the second part. There wasn't any evidence left to be tampered with, really.'

Maurya grins. 'After eleven years in the force, I've learnt to handle those pesky bastards. If you can't convince them, confuse them.' He shakes his head. 'Sit, sit.'

Kiran sits down across from him. Maurya looks up at the television on his left, thankfully on mute. The media has not stopped covering the news of Sanya's arrest and her release since last evening. Maurya knew this would happen. Now, he has the pressure of solving the case, which is getting murkier by the day, and the newshounds are breathing down his neck as well. He didn't want to give them any fodder, but he had done just that.

'DCP Sandhu called me today.' There is a quiver in Maurya's voice. 'He doesn't bother me often. And as

I expected, he wants me to solve the case on priority. There is a lot of media coverage and pressure, and all eyes are on us now. Arresting Sanya pre-emptively backfired.'

'What's our next course of action?'

'Mahesh. He should be with us shortly.'

Fifteen minutes later, they are sitting with Mahesh in the interrogation room. Mahesh appears nervous and his body is tense. He fidgets with his glasses and pushes them up to the bridge of his nose. Maurya watches him for a minute or two before clearing his throat.

'And so, we meet again.'

Mahesh clenches his jaw and does not make a comment.

'I have two simple questions for you,' Maurya starts, glaring at Mahesh. 'Why didn't you tell us earlier that you went back to visit Anant again, this second time through the back door? And second question, why *did* you go the second time?'

'I . . . I forgot to mention it.'

Maurya watches him sceptically, 'Go on.'

'It's . . . it's true. I forgot and I don't even think that it is relevant to the case.'

'But why did you enter through the back door and not through the front?'

'I . . . I . . . well, because my car was parked at the back, and I was already there. I didn't want to take a detour and walk around the entire compound again.'

'And why did you go back?'

Maurya fiddles with his glasses again. 'There was something I forgot to discuss with him.'

'And what was that?'

Here Mahesh blanches noticeably and looks down at the floor. It is clear to Maurya that he might try to concoct an answer and not share the truth.

Mahesh looks up and sighs deeply. 'I went back in to offer him a better deal. I told him that if he merged his fund with my company, I'd offer him much better terms. Although his AUM was still small, it was accelerating fast, and I wanted to benefit from that; at the same time, he would've benefitted from the merger as well.'

'And he neither agreed nor refused your offer?'

'Yes.'

'Hmm,' Maurya considers it. 'Okay, okay. But why were you so desperate to have him on board?'

Mahesh throws him a puzzled look.

'You don't agree?' Maurya picks up a paper. 'These are your phone records. You were hounding him to get back with you. Eighteen calls from your phone to Anant in the last three months, and you get not a single call back! How do you explain that?'

Mahesh feels trapped. His mind is racing now. 'Well, he . . . he was that way, I mean, he liked people calling him and not the other way around. He had an air of superiority about him.'

'Really?'

Mahesh nods, but the conviction is lacking.

'But yesterday you told me that that night of your visit was the first time you asked Anant to collaborate again. So why had you been calling him so much?'

'He was a friend and good at deciphering the stock markets. I liked taking his opinion on where the markets were headed.'

'I see,' Maurya says and rises. He steps towards Mahesh and stands behind him. Kiran has narrowed her eyes at Maurya, wondering what he is up to. Mahesh's heart is hammering hard against his rib cage. He cannot see Maurya, and he does not know whether Maurya believes him or not; he doesn't think so. He didn't sound very convincing.

Maurya places his strong arms on Mahesh's shoulders and the latter shudders.

'My friend,' says Maurya, 'I'm having a hard time believing you. I don't think that was the day you requested Anant the first time; I think you had been pestering him for the past few months. Since the time Anant left you, your fund was losing its clients to him. I'm certain that you were envious of him; he wasn't really your friend, he was your foe—a professional rival. Would you agree?'

'No, n-no . . .' Mahesh stammers and shakes his head in a wild gesture.

'Let's start from the beginning, then,' Maurya says and returns to his chair. 'I want you to start from the day you first met him to the time you started your company together, when he quit, and what transpired until the last day. Feel free to tell us whatever you know of his relationship with his wife and brother. And—' Maurya pounds his fist on the table, 'no lies this time!'

Mahesh recoils a little at the loud tone. He gathers himself slowly, adjusts his glasses again and begins talking.

PART—3

MAHESH MURTHY'S STORY

SIXTEEN

I first met Anant back in 2009 when the global economy was just coming out of a deep recession. The atmosphere was gloomy with soaring bankruptcies, high unemployment rates, reserve banks of the world reducing interest rates and governments printing money to finance their expenditure. Those days, you would not find one optimistic investment professional who believed that the economy and the markets would turn around the way they did.

Well, except Anant Kapoor.

He had joined my team few months ago. I was the fund manager of the biggest asset management company in India and directly in charge of its global equity portfolio. Anant was reporting to me, and part of his job was to track the global macroeconomic climate.

To this day, I am not sure what exactly went through his mind when he approached me one Monday afternoon that year.

'I think we should cover our short positions and start buying massively,' he told me assertively.

I looked at him in astonishment. We were all negative on the market and had taken a short position—basically betting on the market to go down—and here comes this twenty-something amateur and tells me to change our strategy.

'What makes you say that?' I asked, genuinely curious.

He threw a few numbers at me. His confidence in his thesis was extraordinary. I dismissed him outright and asked him to prepare a report on a different subject.

Two weeks later, the markets bottomed and never saw those levels again. It was insane. We had missed a huge buying opportunity. I was extremely agitated with myself for not having been able to spot the obvious, albeit in hindsight.

Anant never gloated about his prescient call about the turnaround, but he made it a point to snub me for not listening to him that entire year. He eventually got promoted and was handed the responsibility of a separate fund within the company. He wasn't my subordinate any more, but we would still liaise and discuss the markets regularly. We became close friends, and I was always amazed at his foresight.

Most people have peripheral knowledge of a subject which they do not study in depth. Anant not only had a deep and holistic view of the investment business, but he was a multidisciplinary learner. He was a voracious reader and he read very widely. All things in the world connect. Apart from business and finance, he was competent in behavioural psychology, macroeconomics and history. That was the reason he was the best investor I'd ever known.

A few years later, he got married. I never met his first wife, and unfortunately she died in a car accident a year into their marriage. Anant was devastated at first, but then later, he submersed himself in work. He was the first person to step into the office and the last to step out. He became a workaholic, sharply improving his foresight of the market and returns of the fund that he was managing. It was unnatural for him to work the way he did, although his bosses never complained, and he rose in the company ranks further.

Here, I can admit that shreds of jealousy started creeping into my psyche, uninvited, like weeds in a garden. I was not aware of it at first, but every other day, when I saw the top bosses in our firm walk over to his cubicle, spend hours with him and exalt him in front of everyone, something started tugging at my heart.

Yes, I was jealous of him, but so was every other fund manager in the company. But that does not mean I would kill him. How could I? I was in awe of the man. He was so good at his work; he had a foresight that was incredible. He managed to call the top and the bottom of the market with amazing regularity. There was so much to learn from him, never mind that he was five years younger and a former subordinate. In our business, you cannot survive if you have an inflated ego. The markets will decimate you. We have always been taught that markets are supreme, and one must respect them.

Towards the end of that year, when his wife passed away, he decided to quit the company and venture out on his own. I had an entrepreneurial streak in me, and I always wanted to work for myself, but I lacked the courage. When Anant told me about his plans, I offered to start a company together with him. Anant accepted the offer with alacrity. So, although it was my idea to start the company together, Anant was equally enthused. Our bosses offered Anant a partnership in the company to deter his decision, but thankfully, Anant had made up his mind.

It was all hunky-dory in the beginning. Since we had a reputation in the industry, it was not difficult to get clients to invest their money. We hardly spent any money on marketing; clients were lining up at our door just by word of mouth. I was aware that Anant was the real star and he attracted most of the capital, but I held my ego in check; I had accepted that he was a far better investor than I could ever be.

Then, a year later, the taunts started coming. They were subtle at first, but gradually, they turned incisive and contemptuous. Perhaps he had started regretting his decision of having a partner in his fund, or perhaps he liked mocking people whom he regarded his inferior. I agree that some of my bets did not do well and brought our internal rate of return down, but that happens with every investor time and again.

For instance, I had invested in an auto ancillaries company that sold automotive parts to various domestic and international car companies. The investment went well for a few months, rising 20 per cent in a short span of time, but it went nowhere over the next few months and then started declining sharply thereafter due to a global slowdown in the automotive industry. Anant suggested we close the position, but I was sure that demand would return, restoring the fortunes of the company. It didn't, and the company's stock plunged 30 per cent from our purchase price. I had to close the position at a big loss.

And what did Anant do? He lambasted me. It is not like he never made mistakes, oh he did, lots of times. But he was very flexible and quick to correct them. He would not have lost so much money in one position and that irked him. To an extent he was right, but hey, we all make mistakes. You've got to be respectful towards people, especially your partners.

That was the day when the cracks in our partnership began appearing. It went downhill from there. Over the next few months, he would scrutinize all my positions as if I were working under him, not with him. Our strategies were also different. He would patiently wait for the stocks to come to him, wait until the risk-reward aligned perfectly; I was more of a go-getter, wanting to be part of the action all the time.

Anant remarried about a year after his first wife passed away. I met Sanya in our office. Anant had invited her to meet with the team. I remember Anant and I had an extremely hard time explaining to her what we did for a living. She was not a finance person at all and very poor with numbers. For some reason, Anant wanted her to understand, or at least get the gist of investing. She hardly took any interest in investing and would stroll around the office quipping that it was too tiny, the walls too shoddy and the furniture very outdated. I found her extremely pleasant and friendly and was happy for Anant. They appeared so much in love, holding hands, cracking jokes and teasing each other.

I am single by choice, but that day, I secretly hankered for a life partner like her. Afterwards, we went out for lunch to an Italian restaurant near our office. I do not remember meeting her again until their first wedding anniversary, and Anant barely spoke about her in the office.

Almost two years into our partnership, it was getting very difficult to work together due to our dissimilitude and Anant decided to part ways. He sold his stake in the company to me and decided to start his own fund. I requested him a few times to reconsider his decision, but he was a headstrong man, and I could not change his mind.

It is true that some of my clients withdrew their capital from my fund and went to Anant, but getting access to sufficient capital from investors to keep his firm profitable was not a walk in the park even for him. It is never easy for any entrepreneur to get off the ground, and Anant was no exception. The problem was that he was good at investing, but not at personal relationships. He would not go out, wine and dine with potential clients and disarm them to get their capital; no, they had to come to him. Call it arrogance or self-assurance, I'm not sure. He was an investing prodigy but a terrible salesperson. He needed me to get the clients for him.

It was also true that, despite the lack of his sales pitches, the assets under his management were increasing, but not at a pace that he would have hoped. It was probably clear to him that both of us were better off together. Complementing each other's skills always works in business.

Anant had another problem. His brother. Vicky was an inveterate gambler and having first blown away his share of their father's wealth, he was on to Anant's money. Anant would be furious with him and some days we had long talks on how Vicky had turned out the way he did, I mean so different from his brother. There are some gamblers who are actually good at what they do. They master the art of identifying the correct risk-reward and bet only when they are satisfied that the conditions are in their favour. They think like a casino, not a gambler. But not Vicky. He was a pathetic gambler; he'd bet blindly with no sense of probabilities or odds. He was addicted, he just had to bet. And heavily. The bids were in crores of rupees. Anant told me recently that Vicky owed a bookie about two crore rupees and that he was threatening Vicky. Can you believe that? He had the gall to lie to his brother so he could fleece more money out of him. At least that's what Anant told me, that he did not believe Vicky's story, that it was made up.

Vicky would often argue that Anant had enough money and so what if he lost some of it; he was family, after all. Anant realized that Vicky was the proverbial small leak that could sink a great ship. Anant had mentioned to me once in passing that even his wife, Sanya, was a spendthrift. Both his brother and wife loved an opulent lifestyle, buying fancy cars, dining in expensive restaurants, et al., whereas Anant was sort of a miser. He would spend his money, no doubt, but he preferred accumulating wealth and, as far as possible, spending only on necessities. He was a value buyer and had a similar outlook when it came to investing in businesses, which was probably the reason he was so successful in investing.

I realized that Anant had enough wealth, but it was depleting. And here I sensed an opportunity. It was likely that when I approached him to get back together, if my timing was right, the odds were high that he would agree. And so, that day, I called him and asked to spend the evening together.

I've been telling the truth that it was the first time that I brought up the topic of collaborating again that night, and Anant told me that he would consider it. I went back into that house the second time, this time through the back door, to revise my terms and give him a better deal. I wanted him back; yes, I agree, I was desperate; but why would I kill him?

The next morning, I heard the news of his murder.

SEVENTEEN

Before letting Mahesh go, Maurya made him sign his statement and warned him that if he had lied, his statement would be used against him in court. Mahesh nodded, signed the document and fled the station in a jiffy.

After he left, Maurya made a few phone calls. He called up Mahesh's company and jotted down the names and numbers of the employees who knew Mahesh and Anant well. He repeated the exercise with Anant's company and then with the company where they had worked together. He'd have to speak with more people and get an unbiased view of their relationship. One man is dead and the other, a liar.

'I think what he told us makes sense, right?' Kiran says, putting the receiver of the telephone down on Maurya's desk.

'Why?'

'I mean if he needed Anant, why would he kill him?'

'He could be lying,' Maurya replies flatly. 'That story could be fabricated. Who knows? Never take statements from an accused at face value.'

Kiran nods, feeling a little sheepish.

'Listen to everyone,' Maurya continues in an assertive tone, 'but trust no one. Sanya told us that Mahesh had begged Anant to start the company together whereas in Mahesh's version, Anant accepted the offer with alacrity. So, either he is lying or Sanya is lying. Or maybe both are lying.' Maurya shakes his head. 'We don't know that yet. Then we have the brother who owes two crores to a bookie which might have been a motive.' He sighs in frustration.

Kiran nods again.

It's been more than seventy-two hours since Anant's dead body was found, and they still don't have any substantial leads. The case is going nowhere, and she is sure her boss must be feeling the pressure to solve it quickly. The media continues pursuing the case unabated, tightening the noose further.

Maurya looks down at the diary that is open in front of him. They have managed to secure the names and contact numbers of four people who knew Mahesh and Anant well. For the rest of the morning and afternoon, they have set up meetings with them.

Maurya is desperate for a breakthrough. Sometimes it is little clues, small conversations with irrelevant people, an innocuous remark by the accused that can help resolve a complex case. So far, he has nothing. It is day four after the murder and he realizes he must move fast.

He gets to his feet and collects the keys of his jeep from the desk. 'Let's go.'

'I am Joe Mascarenhas, a friend of Mahesh, and I also knew Anant well. Yes, it is true that Mahesh had come to my place that night for a few drinks and left after an hour.'

'How did you know them?'

'The three of us worked in Fidelity Group, although in different departments. Mahesh had introduced me to Anant. He was a star in the company.'

'Were they close?'

'Yes, I think so. They started a company together.'

'Do you know whose idea it was to start the company together?'

'Both, I think."

'Then why did they separate?'

'Well, I guess difference of opinion.'

'Do you know Mahesh was requesting Anant to get back together?'

'Yes, Mahesh had told me that recently. But what is the problem with that? It's always good to have the smartest people in your team.'

'Do you think he could've killed Anant?'

'Of course not! They were good friends.'

'Thank you.'

'My name is Sourabh Banerjee. I was in the same team as Anant, and we reported to Mahesh.'

'What did you think about Anant?'

'He was brilliant. Such a shocker to know that he got killed.'

'Do you think Mahesh could have killed him?'

'I . . . I don't know.'

'They started a company together. Do you know whose idea it was?'

'I think both, but it always surprised me that Anant would want to work with Mahesh.'

'Why would it surprise you?'

'I mean Anant was very good in investing, and Mahesh was . . . well, let's just say that he isn't the smartest investor around. It made a lot of sense to me when Anant separated and started his own company.'

'So could it have been that it was Mahesh who proposed the partnership to Anant to start a company together in those days?'

'Yes definitely. It could have never been the other way around.'

'Thank you.'

'My name is Jay, and I knew Anant sir very well. I was an analyst at Fidelity and working under him. A few years later, he called me out of the blue and offered me a position in his company. It was the happiest day of my life. Anant sir was my mentor.'

'And Mahesh?'

'I never liked him. He wasn't really a finance guy; he was just good at licking the asses of the bosses, if you know what I mean.'

'Can you elaborate further?'

'I mean he was more of a marketer and salesperson, really. He was good at soliciting people and getting access to their capital, but not at investing. In fact, he was a shameless cloner; he'd copy the ideas of other, more qualified, investors, and simply ape them. He was nowhere as adept in reading the market as Anant sir.'

'Do you know if Mahesh was begging Anant to collaborate again?'

'I . . . I wouldn't know that, but come on, of course he would want that. Everybody wanted Anant sir on his side. And especially Mahesh.'

'So, could he have been begging Anant?'

'Oh, absolutely. And Mahesh had no shame or self-respect. It wouldn't have mattered to him that Anant sir had left him in the first place.'

'Do you think Mahesh could have killed him?'

'Oh, I have no idea about that. Mahesh didn't seem like a violent person at all.'

'Thank you very much.'

'I am Soumya Kriplani. I am an accountant at Mahesh's company.'

'How well do you know Mahesh?'

'I've been working under him for three years now.'

'And what is he like?'

'He's a nice gentleman. He treats his employees very well.'

'And Anant? Did you know him?'

'Yes. He was a partner at this company, but he quit about a year ago.'

'And how was he?'

'He was okay. I think Mahesh and Anant were friends from a previous company, but I could never understand their relationship.'

'What do you mean?'

'I mean, although they were equal partners at the firm, Anant was always bossing Mahesh around. Mahesh would take orders from him as though he worked under him. And some days, Anant would be very rude. Not just to Mahesh, but to the other employees as well. When he was angry, his face would become bright red and a vein would pop out right in the centre of his forehead. The other employees would hide behind their computer screens to escape his wrath.'

'I see. And Mahesh would never retaliate?'

'Never. He was a sissy. I think he feared Anant.'

'Why?'

'He needed Anant more than Anant needed him.'

'But Anant eventually left.'

'Yes, he did. Since I handle the accounts, I know that the capital slowly started dwindling with his exit.'

'Would it surprise you to know that Mahesh would beg to get Anant back?'

'Not at all. Like I said, Anant was running the show here, and Mahesh and our fund have definitely suffered from Anant's departure.'

'Do you think Mahesh could have killed him?'

'Why would he kill him? He needed Anant.'

'It could have been a mistake.'

'I'm sorry, I have no idea about that.'

'Thank you.'

EIGHTEEN

It is crystal-clear to Maurya now that Mahesh has been lying all along. He needed Anant to be his business partner and had wheedled and coaxed him until Anant gave in. It wouldn't have taken Anant long to realize that Mahesh hardly added any value to the business except, of course, flattering the customers. Anant couldn't tolerate Mahesh's ineptitude, so he had decided to split and start his own company. Then Mahesh urged him again, this time more desperately than before, as he was losing his clients.

That night, Mahesh might have been overcome by despair when Anant rebuffed his offer. But would he kill Anant for that? Maurya cannot answer that with certainty. Even if he can, he doesn't have any evidence or witnesses to support his claim. No court would prosecute an accused based on vacuous conjecture.

After speaking with the various people involved, Maurya has formed a mental picture of Anant—that of a brilliant, devoted worker, phenomenal at his job, and who expected nothing but the best from the people around him. Like his own self. Alas, that was not the case! Not the wife, or the brother, or the friend, if he could call Mahesh that. All three of them, the three suspects, were nothing like Anant. They were poles apart.

All Anant got was a gambler and irresponsible brother; an extravagant and hare-brained wife who hadn't a clue about how her husband earned a living; and an incompetent but beguiling investor friend. No wonder they made Anant furious, and he snapped at them on various occasions. He was a brilliant man surrounded by mediocrity.

But Maurya is still not certain who killed Anant or the motive behind the crime, although he feels in his gut that he is getting close. The killer would fumble and provide him that essential clue sooner than later. They all invariably fumble. Thus far it could be any one of the three, either unaided or with the help of an accomplice. He needs to continue investigating.

Along with Kiran, Maurya is on his way to New Delhi. He wants to have a quick word with Vicky's friend, Navid, his alibi for the night of the murder. He had Kiran inform Navid of their visit beforehand to ensure that he was home.

Navid's apartment is in the southern part of the city, close to the border. After getting off the expressway, Maurya takes a right and follows the road. He passes a slew of makeshift shops to his left and heads straight until he hits an intersection, then turns right again. He enters an old neighbourhood and the difference with the millennium city is unmistakable. The paint on the walls of the derelict building which they approach is flaking, with several marks on the walls where hasty repairs have been made. There is a small park opposite the building, but it is bereft of greenery and there are rusted swings for the kids on one side. Maurya parks his car along the side of the park and gets out of the jeep. *Strange that a rich lad like Vicky has friends in such a shoddy neighbourhood as this*, he thinks, looking up.

'What a dump,' Kiran remarks quietly.

An old man with a load of bricks neatly stacked on top of his head ambles past them.

Maurya walks towards the entrance and looks at the note in his hand. 'Unit 213 is on the third floor.' There is a concrete stairwell to their left and Maurya starts towards it. Kiran follows him.

As soon as they're outside the apartment, down the hall, furthest from the stairwell, Maurya rings the doorbell. The door swings open a crack, the door chain still attached. A middle-aged woman peers through the opening at the two officers suspiciously. 'Yes?'

'We're here to meet Navid,' Maurya tells the woman through the door gently. 'We had called.'

The woman nods and closes the door, undoes the chain and opens the door wide. Maurya and Kiran step into the tiny apartment.

'Take a seat,' the woman says, showing them to the tacky, red-coloured couch in the middle of the room. 'I'll call Navid from the back.'

'Thank you.'

Maurya sits down and looks around the room casually. It is less than a minute and he is already feeling claustrophobic. There are no windows in sight and the low-watt bulb in the centre of the wall to his left emits insufficient light. The fan overhead spins in lazy circles, hardly throwing out any air. At the far end, the open kitchen appears to be in a mess with utensils strewn all over the kitchen's counters. He looks over his shoulder and notes a narrow passageway—perhaps a balcony—leading to another room. A tall, lanky man saunters towards them.

'Hello, sir, I'm Navid,' he offers his hand.

Maurya takes it and gives a firm handshake. 'Hello. I'm inspector Maurya, and this is sub-inspector Kiran.'

'Yes,' Navid says, sitting down on a flimsy plastic chair opposite them. 'She called me earlier.'

'Okay, good,' Maurya starts, moving uncomfortably on the couch. 'I want you to tell me how long you've known Vicky and how well you know him.'

'About nine years now. We graduated together from Deshbandhu College, and we are good friends. We meet often and he usually picks me up from outside my apartment.'

'And when did you meet him last?'

Navid narrows his eyes and thinks about it for a moment. 'On . . . on Sunday, four days ago.'

'Where?'

'We went to a bar in Vasant Vihar.'

'Do you remember what time you left?'

'I . . . I do not remember exactly, but I think it was around midnight.'

Maurya consults his diary and nods. It should be fifteen minutes from this place to the toll bridge, so it makes sense as Vicky's car was caught by the cameras there at 12.15. He can always check the cameras at the bar to be doubly sure, but he doubts he will need to do that. For now, he believes Vicky's story. So far so good.

'Sorry, would you like to have some water,' Navid offers politely. 'I forgot to ask.'

Kiran waves casually. 'No, thank you. We're good.'

'Tell me, Navid, what were you guys talking about that day?'

Navid stiffens perceptibly at Maurya's question. He lowers his eyes, and Maurya can sense that, for the first time in the conversation, he is suddenly ill at ease.

'Please tell me in detail,' Maurya adds. 'I think your statement is very important to the case.'

Navid looks up and bites his lips. 'I . . . I think you already know.'

'We want to hear it from you.'

Navid takes a deep breath and runs a hand across his face. 'Vicky, he . . . he was very tense as a bookie to whom he owed money, money which he had lost in a bet, had been threatening him. As you know, the IPL season is on and although illegal, um . . . people still bet on matches all the time.'

'D'you bet as well?'

Navid freezes and his eyes are now wide open. 'Um, er—'

Maurya chuckles softly. 'I don't care. Tell me what happened next.'

'I told him to ask his brother for the money, but he was very scared of him. When he was staking such a huge amount, I had warned him, but he was so drunk that he just made a call and, without a second thought, picked his team and the amount. I told him to go to his brother, beg, borrow, whatever, but get the money because this bookie would not let him go easy.'

'Do you know the bookie?'

'No, no, I don't know,' Navid replies, shaking his head. 'Nobody knows him. He's a ghost. No one has seen him. We don't even know his name. All we know is that he's an extremely influential man, hobnobbing with the city's elite, and that you do not mess with him. If you win, you'll get your cash delivered the next day to your doorstep, and if you lose, you ought to come up with it. No excuses. He is very fair that way.'

'Yes, very fair,' Maurya grunts. 'And what did Vicky do?'

'He begged for a few more days. He told the bookie's men that he was arranging for the cash.'

Maurya and Kiran share a quick glance.

'Did he ever speak to Anant,' Kiran asks, 'um, his brother, and ask for the money?'

'Yes, he did,' Navid replies, nodding, looking at Kiran now. 'But his brother never believed him and shooed him away.'

Maurya sits back on the couch and considers it. So, Vicky really did need that money. In Mahesh's version, Anant didn't believe that Vicky had lost the bet and a bookie was harassing him. Or maybe Mahesh was lying. Sanya had also mentioned about the bookie, so Vicky must've been telling the truth. He had another line of thought. If Vicky really needed the money, what good would it do for him to kill Anant? He loses his brother, but he still does not get the money.

'Is there anything else that you would like to share with us?' Maurya asks.

'All I know is that Vicky was extremely edgy, and he wanted to get that bookie off his back. The constant calls were tormenting him.'

'Did he ever get those calls when he was with you?'

'Yes, yes, absolutely.'

'And did the bookie call directly?'

'No, no.' Navid shakes his head. 'His goons would call. The last call was, I think, a week ago; Vicky was told that they would chop off his legs if they didn't get the money in ten days.'

Maurya blinks. 'Whaaat?'

'Yes. And, despite that, his brother didn't believe him.'

'Do you have the number that the calls came from?' Maurya asked, then waved his hand. 'Actually, let it be. I'll ask Vicky that question.'

'No point,' Navid says. 'All the calls were from untraceable numbers.'

'But how was Vicky contacting them to place his bets?'

'Oh, for that there is just one number.' Navid pulls out his phone from the pocket of his trousers. 'I can give you that.' He flicks through the screen. 'Ah, here it is.'

Maurya jots down the number.

'We give just one ring, then disconnect and we get a call back from an unknown caller. If you exceed the one ring, you won't get a call back.'

Maurya grimaces. 'Okay, noted.' He turns to Kiran who looks blankly back at him. 'Right. I don't think I have any more questions for now.' He gets to his feet and walks to the door. 'Thank you.'

After they have stepped outside, Kiran's face is twisted in confusion.

'What?' says Maurya, flicking his brow.

'Could it be that bookie?'

NINETEEN

Sanya is in the kitchen when the doorbell rings. She looks up at the wall clock. 7.30 p.m. *Finally, he's home.*

'Let me take a look,' she tells Sharda, who is seated on the floor, kneading dough in a large bowl, her hands messy. She walks down the long hallway and heads to the door. The doorbell rings again.

'Where have you been all day?' she hisses after opening the door.

A visibly inebriated Vicky staggers in, his jacket tucked in the crook of his left elbow. He gives Sanya a cold, hard look, does not reply and walks past her.

'Vicky,' she calls to his retreating back, 'has the bookie contacted you?'

Vicky stops in his tracks, then pivots on his heels. 'Why do you care now?' His voice is loud and raspy.

Sanya scowls and takes a step forward. 'Excuse me?'

Vicky rolls his eyes. 'I told you this was serious, but you didn't help me.'

Now Sanya rolls her eyes. Sometimes she doesn't understand her brother-in-law at all. 'I asked you to speak with Anant.'

'And do you think he ever listened to me?'

'Well, that makes two of us.'

'But you were his wife. Of course he would've listened to you.'

'And you were his brother, dumbo!'

Vicky puts a hand to his head and sighs. He looks tired, dishevelled and very pale. He has not shaved for the past week, and he desperately needs a haircut. It doesn't look like he has combed his hair in days. His paunch is sticking out from beneath his T-shirt which is tucked untidily into his green linen pants.

He flops down on the sofa and stoops forward, clutching his forehead in distress. Sanya sits beside him and places her hand on his lap.

'It's all my fault, you know,' he mutters under his breath.

'No, you're right,' Sanya says slowly. 'I . . . I should've spoken to Anant on your behalf. Or perhaps I should have lent you my money.'

There is a long pause. Vicky shakes his head slowly from side to side. 'Too late.'

'You . . . d'you think . . .' she cringes in pain and puckers her face in contempt. 'Anant was killed because of—'

'I . . . I don't know.' He pulls out his phone and unlocks the screen. He flicks through the messages. 'They're not contacting me any more. Why?'

The doorbell rings again and it sends a shiver through them. Sanya looks up at the wall clock again. *Who could it be this time?* She rises and heads for the door. She looks through the peephole. It is that inspector again. What does he want now?

'It's them again,' Sanya mutters to Vicky, who sits up and runs a hand through his hair. He tucks the T-shirt properly into his pants and sits up straight.

'Hello, Mrs Kapoor,' Maurya says softly when Sanya swings the door open. 'We're very sorry to barge in unannounced at this time.'

'What do you want now?' Sanya asks impatiently. She doesn't bother to hide her displeasure.

Maurya doesn't feel offended. *She has a right to be miffed*, he thinks. Four days gone and he still hasn't caught the killer. To make matters worse, he arrested her rather impulsively. He leans forward and glances sideways at Vicky. 'We just want to have a quick chat with your brother-in-law.'

Sanya glares and does not let them in for a few moments. Then she moves aside. 'Okay, come on in.'

'Thank you, Mrs Kapoor.' He steps in and Kiran follows him. The two women exchange a quick glance. Maurya starts for the couch, then stops and looks over his shoulder. 'Mrs Kapoor, we do not have any questions for you. You may retire to your bedroom. Good night.'

Sanya nods and glances at Vicky. Their eyes meet. She slowly sets off to the stairs in front of her that lead to her bedroom. Maurya's eyes follow her to the stairs, then he sits on a leather chair across from Vicky. Kiran sits beside him on another chair.

'We met your friend Navid today,' Maurya starts. He snaps his fingers at Vicky's obvious inattention. 'Vicky?'

'Sorry, what?'

'We met your friend—'

'Yes, I know.'

Maurya snorts. 'Your friend told us that the bookie's stooges had threatened to chop off your legs. Is that true?'

Vicky lowers his head and slowly nods.

'And when was this?'

'Last week.'

'Exact day, please?'

Vicky grunts. He looks at his phone again. 'It was Thursday.'

'Oh, today is Thursday as well, so seven days ago.' Maurya makes a note. 'And what did they tell you?'

'They gave me ten days' time to arrange for the money.'

'Which expires in three days' time.'

Vicky rubs his eyes. They are as red as cherries. Either he hasn't been sleeping or he weeps all day. 'I know, I know . . .' he trails off and stares into the distance, a look of horror clouding his face. 'But they haven't been—they haven't contacted me since—'

'Since your brother's murder,' Maurya completes the sentence for him.

'Yes.'

Maurya scratches his nose. 'Do you think it could have been his henchmen who would have killed your—'

Vicky shakes his head. 'I don't know. I have been, um, thinking about it as well.'

'Are you saying they might have settled the score with your brother?'

Vicky shrugs.

Maurya continues after a moment when an answer is not forthcoming from Vicky, 'You told me earlier that you had asked your brother for the money and that he refused to give it to you. Then, in your phone records, I see that you made a call to your brother,' he consults his notes, 'at 10.55 p.m. What did you speak about?'

'Same thing,' Vicky replies, anger creeping into his voice. 'I again asked him for the money. I begged him. I told him about the bookie's warning. In fact, I also promised him that I would stop betting after settling this last score.'

'And he refused again?'

'Yes,' Vicky replies firmly.

'Okay.' Maurya consults his diary again. 'I also see that you and your sister-in-law exchanged sixty-eight calls in the last three months. What were they about?'

Vicky blushes and bites his lip nervously. Maurya is gazing at him intently. He is very keen to hear Vicky's explanation. Sanya had told him that they spoke about his gambling and that he should get rid of it, the bookie's money, the ebb and flow of the relationship with his brother and that he must work to improve it. What would Vicky say?

'I'm waiting,' Maurya says, glaring at him impatiently.

'Well, lots of things,' Vicky starts slowly, returning Maurya's gaze. 'She's my sounding board. I bounce all my thoughts off her. Ideally, that should have been my brother, but I was always scared of Anant. In fact, she was sort of a shield against all my brother's tirades. I . . . I think that my brother despised me and . . . and Sanya always wanted us to be close again. As I already told you last time, we were not on talking terms for the past few months. Sanya told me repeatedly to quit gambling, which I had planned to do, and she urged me to sort out all the differences with my brother, but then—'

'But then?'

Vicky stares directly at Maurya' face. 'But then he died, what else?'

'Murdered,' Maurya corrects him, raising a minatory index finger. 'He was murdered. Someone killed him.'

Vicky turns pale and swallows. 'Yes, right.'

Maurya purses his lips, nods his head slowly, and continues glowering at Vicky. He is still not able to decipher whether he is disturbed by his brother's death. There is hardly a shred of emotion underpinning his expression. Either that, or the man is impassive by nature. Or he is a good actor.

Maurya clears his throat. 'There is one more thing I wanted to quickly tick off my list.' When he has Vicky's attention, he continues as gently as possible, without setting off any alarms, 'Did your brother have a will?'

Vicky shrugs and shakes his head. 'Not that I'm aware of.'

'Who gets all of Anant's money now?'

Again, a blank. Not a shred of emotion. Not a twitch, a frown, a wrinkle. Nothing. He just sits there and looks blankly at Maurya. 'I think, maybe us, Sanya and I. I haven't thought about it.'

Maurya has a smug expression on his face. He smiles quietly. Kiran gives Maurya a sidelong glance and wonders what that is all about. Wasn't this expected?

'Thank you,' Maurya rises. 'I think I have what I wanted. Have a good night.'

'Goodnight.'

TWENTY

The next morning DCP Sandhu summons Maurya to his room. He is a tall, burly, middle-aged Sikh, and by and large, leaves his juniors to operate on their own terms without any interference. The smarter ones, at least. It is his firm belief that it is best to leave the bright people alone to get the best out of them. Do not micromanage them. And fire the others. No need to waste your time on them.

But the murder case of the famous fund manager has forced him to meddle. It has been more than ninety-six hours since the murder and his department has not yet cracked the puzzle. The media does not stop covering the news and, with every passing day, the pressure to resolve the case increases.

When Maurya steps into the room, Sandhu is glowering behind his desk. He acknowledges Maurya's presence and gestures to the chair across from him.

'What's happening, Maurya? Today is the fifth day.'

Maurya sits down. He opens his mouth to speak but does not find an appropriate answer. He looks away.

'I expect better from you.' Sandhu's tone softens. 'You took forty-eight hours to solve cases like these in the past. What's happening this time?'

Maurya nods and looks directly at his superior now. He rubs his face. 'The problem I'm having is the absence of any witness whatsoever. Hardly anything relevant comes up on the CCTV footage in the area as the cameras are far from the victim's bungalow; and the evidence we have is circumstantial, to put it mildly, as the suspect lives in that house, so it is not unusual to have her fingerprints on the murder weapon and more than one motive.'

'Please elaborate.'

Over the next ten minutes or so, Maurya lays out the details of the case. He explains all the information he has unearthed on the case so far.

Sandhu leans back in his chair and thinks pensively for a long moment. 'Were there no unidentified cars or bikes that turned up on that street that night?'

'We cannot say that for sure. There are no CCTV cameras on that street. We checked a few of them installed by the shops but they run perpendicular to that street and were a little further away. We cannot know for sure which ones turned on to that street.'

'But you suspect that the victim knew the killer, so it should be the wife, brother or friend?'

'That's what we believe, yes.'

'Hmm,' Sandhu nods and then says after a beat, 'and that bookie you mentioned? Could he have anything to do with it?'

'Could be. I have asked my team to start finding out more about him. We do not have any leads about him so far.'

'Find out, find out,' Sandhu snaps his fingers. 'Time is running out, Maurya. You should have started working on him earlier.'

Maurya clicks his tongue in frustration. 'I couldn't have known!' he shakes his head, disgruntled. 'It was clear from the get-go that it had to be one of the three suspects, but only now have I been thinking that we may have been barking up the wrong tree.'

Sandhu does not respond immediately. He lets the tension in the air dissipate. Maurya's tone has clearly gone up a notch. Sandhu crosses his arms across his chest and speaks as gently as he can, 'May I ask you, if you were not sure, why did you arrest Sanya in the first place?'

'Because Sanya did not have an alibi. The murder weapon had her fingerprints. The night before the murder, she had had an argument with her husband who then pushed her, causing a minor injury on her head. Tell me if that isn't reasonable grounds for suspicion?'

'Then why did you release her?'

'Because, upon further investigation, I realized that she might not have done it. It could've been the other two suspects.' A look of disenchantment appears on his face. Maurya is shaking his head in obvious annoyance. Then he glances up at Sandhu and comments, 'I know my job, sir. If I've made a mistake, I will accept and correct it, instead of hiding it. You know me. I had to release that woman as I had insufficient evidence against her.'

'Of course, of course, Maurya.' Sandhu rises and goes to Maurya's side, gently patting his shoulder. 'You get offended very quickly. I have to ask these questions; I too report to someone, after all.'

Maurya takes a deep breath and hisses out sharply through his teeth. 'Sorry, sir. I think that I've disappointed you. The fact is that I've disappointed myself. I should've cracked this case by now.'

'Never mind,' Sandhu sits back on his chair. 'Let's give it our best now. Tell me, is there anyone else who lives in that house apart from the brother and the wife?'

'They have a helper.'

'Don't you suspect her?'

Maurya is taken aback. 'No. We didn't find her fingerprints on the murder weapon, and there was no smudge, no sign of tampering whatsoever. Further, she did not have any motive to kill the victim.'

'Okay. Find out more about that bookie then and keep me posted.'

'Of course, sir.' Maurya gets to his feet and heads to the door.

Sandhu calls out. 'Listen, Maurya,' he waits until Maurya turns around and is looking at him, 'don't let any self-doubts creep into your head. You're the best officer I know and I'm sure you'll crack the case soon.'

Maurya nods and exits the room.

Over the rest of the morning, Maurya sits behind his desk poring over the case in minute detail. Has he been missing something? Did he overlook anything obvious? Sometimes the answer is right in front of you, but it's the tendency of human nature to always look for complex solutions. Obvious answers are underrated. He has studied a bit of psychology, and he knows this basic misconception which pervades the very fabric of every investigation.

He pulls out a blank sheet of paper from the drawer and places it on the desk. He picks up a pen and starts by writing the names of the three suspects. One by one, he jots down what he has learnt of them over the past few days. This includes their characteristic traits, motives, alibis, relationship with the victim, whether they stand to gain anything at all from the victim's death and so on.

He tries to remove all prejudices and biases from his thought process and reason as rationally as he can. Sometimes, the accused deliberately feeds inaccurate information to the police to throw them off track, and since the first impression, when lodged in the brain, tends to overpower the latter ones, it is always advisable to look at the case from a fresh perspective. He shuts down that part of his brain which already has all the answers and opens another which is completely barren, thinking about the case anew.

In the list of suspects, he also adds the bookie but after a lot of reasoning, takes him off his list.

TWENTY-ONE

At around midday, when Kiran approaches him there's a spring in her step—she announces that they've managed to ferret out crucial details about the bookie.

Maurya dismisses it.

'Why?' she asks, looking in astonishment at Maurya. 'Just a few hours ago, you asked us to dig out more information about him.'

'Yes,' Maurya nods thoughtfully. 'But just think about this rationally. If you were the bookie and the only way to get the money was Vicky's brother, why would you kill him?'

'I . . . I don't know,' she snorts. 'Maybe because I was pissed that I wasn't getting my money.'

'Yes, okay. But when you gave Vicky ten days to get the money, which was last Thursday, why kill his brother on Sunday, three days later, without giving him a chance to return the money? Does it make any sense?'

Kiran sits down. Clearly, she hadn't thought of that. She drums her fingers on the desk, holding Maurya's gaze. 'No, it doesn't.'

A wry smile appears on Maurya's face. He places his elbows on the desk and props his chin on his hands. 'Of course it doesn't.' He clicks his tongue. 'Stop wasting your time on that bookie.'

'But if he didn't get the money from Vicky, why has he stopped hounding him?'

'His brother is killed, Kiran!' Maurya snaps, his eyes glinting intensely. 'Come on! Think logically. Why would the bookie want to draw unnecessary attention to himself? His money can wait.'

Kiran's lips curl in a sneer.

'And I've eliminated Mahesh as well,' Maurya adds, with an air of finality. 'I don't think he could've killed Anant.'

A look of bewilderment comes into Kiran's eyes. She frowns. 'Why not?'

'Because he's left-handed,' Maurya replies flatly. 'That's why I made him sign a paper when he was here, to be sure.'

Kiran recalls that she had been surprised when Maurya had asked for a signature that day, because the interrogation room had a camera and the entire conversation had been recorded. It seemed pointless at the time. Now she knows the reason.

'See, Anant's body was lying right in front of his desk. The wooden cabinet with all the artefacts and showpieces was behind him. The killer would've picked up the murder weapon—that blue copper vase—from there and struck Anant. It seems Anant was standing facing that cabinet when the killer struck him—unless the killer moved the body after the job, which isn't likely. What was the need? Recall that there is hardly any place between the desk and the cabinet so it is likely that the killer, during his strike, stood in a straight line or a little to the right of Anant.' Maurya pauses and watches Kiran intently, hoping that she would comprehend his line of reasoning by now. He knows this is conjecture, but if he cannot identify the killer, he must eliminate the suspects one at a time.

Kiran is wearing an intense expression on her face. She glances up at Maurya. 'The injury was on the left of the victim's forehead, so . . .' she trails off, now connecting the theory.

'Exactly!' Maurya says with an excited chuckle. 'How can a left-hander standing in the same line or to the right of the victim blow a strike on the left side of the forehead?'

'And it was a pretty sharp blow, I remember.' Kiran recalls the sight of the victim when she first saw him.

Maurya nods, raising his eyebrows. He retracts his arms and leans back in his chair, slowly oscillating it, still mulling over his new-found theory; the chair emits a sharp squeak every time he turns right. 'But I'm not very sure about it . . .' he mutters half to himself. 'The reason is that Mahesh had such a strong reason to get rid of Anant. They couldn't have been friends, for sure;

professional rivals can hardly be friends. There is always the possibility that he could've still done it; I mean, what if Anant was looking to his right, then Mahesh could have still struck him where he did, irrespective of where he stood . . .' he pauses, and then another thought strikes him, 'but then, there is another reason because of which I'm inclined to think that he couldn't have done it.'

'What is that?'

'See, Mahesh claims he left that house at 11 p.m. and was at his friend's house ten or fifteen minutes after that, which his friend also corroborates. Forensics have narrowed down the time of death between 11 p.m. and 12.30 a.m. Let's assume that Mahesh killed Anant at 11 p.m. and then left the house; would he just need ten to fifteen minutes to rush out of the house, change into a fresh shirt—for sure the old shirt would be splattered with some blood—and drive to his friend's house which is at least a six- to seven-minute drive away? Then act completely normal in front of his friend so he doesn't suspect anything amiss?' Maurya shakes his head. 'I don't think so. I mean, not if you're a first-time killer, no. He would've been shaking after the murder. It would've taken him ten minutes just to calm down, don't you think so?'

Kiran scratches her forehead, staring off into distance, carefully considering it. After a few moments of rumination her vision regains focus, and she meets Maurya's gaze. 'I think you're right. He might not have done it.'

'Yes, "might" being the operative word, as I'm not ruling him out completely.'

'And what about the other two?'

Maurya stops moving his chair. 'Let's start with the brother first. If I were to tell you that this whole story of the bookie was fabricated, would you believe me?'

'Whaaat?'

'No, no,' Maurya laughs. 'I'm not saying it is. My point being, if you remove the bookie from the picture, would you still suspect the brother?'

Kiran narrows her eyes and glances at her superior in surprise. 'I can't understand where you want to go with this?'

Maurya sighs. 'What I mean is that if there was no bookie we wouldn't have suspected Vicky, would we? We've been assuming all along that since he needed the money, he could've killed his brother. Then again, why kill his brother if he needed the money? But let's keep all that aside for now and look at the big picture. With Anant's death, does Vicky get a dime of his brother's wealth? I asked him yesterday, but that dumbass doesn't even know this. Anant had left no will, and in its absence, his sister-in-law gets the entire estate as per the Hindu Succession Act. So why kill his brother?'

Kiran purses her lips, nodding quietly.

'But then his alibi doesn't hold much water, if you ask me,' Maurya continues, wrinkling his forehead in apparent confusion, looking away. 'He was in the house during the murder, and the very fact that he lied to us about the time of his return, suggests foul play to me. I'm convinced, though, that the death of his brother benefitted him in no way, at least not directly. He might not have killed his brother, but either he was an accomplice or was somehow involved. The brothers weren't on talking terms for the past few months . . . that itself doesn't go down well with me.'

'And that leaves us with the wife,' Kiran spells out, shooting her superior a piercing glance.

'Yes, the wife,' Maurya says in a low voice, nodding mechanically. He straightens up and crosses his arms. 'She confounds me. Why would she kill her husband? And if she did, why would she not plan an alibi and clean up the murder weapon? Is she really that stupid? Or perhaps . . . she killed him accidentally?'

'Accidentally?' Kiran echoes in a sombre tone.

'I mean she might not have had a motive, but she killed him by, um, mistake. Recall, the husband and wife had a fight on the day of the murder, and he had pushed or hit her. What if the fight got out of control and—' he shakes his head, tutting a few times. 'No, it can't be. After the fight, Anant spent a few hours with Mahesh. It's unlikely that after Mahesh left, they resumed their fight and then she killed him.'

'And also, she had her flight tickets for Dehradun booked,' Kiran reminds him.

'Yes, there's that.'

A silence falls between them for the next few minutes. Maurya knows that there is some crucial link that he's still missing—like a jigsaw puzzle which cannot be solved until all the pieces fall in place. One or at the most two pieces are still missing. But the problem is that he doesn't know where to look. Or what to look for.

He decides that he needs to know more about the suspects. He needs to do some more digging.

Tentatively, he picks up his mobile phone from the desk and dials a number. Kiran is peering at him from across the desk.

'Hello, Mrs Kapoor? Inspector Maurya . . . I would like to speak with you further . . . yes . . . today, please . . . at the station . . . thank you.'

Kiran tilts her head and narrows her eyes at Maurya. 'What do you have in mind?'

'You'll see.'

TWENTY-TWO

Sanya arrives at the station less than an hour later. She is in traditional Indian clothes, a dull salwar suit, and barely any make-up.

Maurya greets her amicably and leads her to the interrogation room. Kiran doesn't join them; Maurya wants her to continue digging out more information on the bookie. Even if he isn't behind the murder, the information gathered might help them understand Vicky's involvement, if at all.

Sanya sits down on the wobbly chair gingerly and casts a quick glance around the room. She is familiar with this place and wonders what new questions the inspector has for her now. Her heart races as Maurya takes a seat across from her. She flicks a glance at the camera to her right.

'Yes,' Maurya starts, 'as you're probably aware, our conversation will be recorded.'

Sanya nods. 'What do you want to ask me now? I already told you everything, inspector.'

Maurya gives her a half-smile. 'Honestly, I don't have any questions for you.' He scratches his nose. 'I just want you to listen to me today.'

Sanya feels the tension growing within her. She doesn't like the look on Maurya's face.

'Today is the fifth day of the murder and I'm very disappointed with myself that I haven't managed to solve this crime yet. As you're aware, there are three suspects in this case: Mahesh, Vicky and yourself. Those two have alibis—not watertight, I must add—but you don't. Those two have motives but you don't, although the evidence is pointing against you. A little confusing, don't you think?'

Sanya feels her jaw clench involuntarily. She doesn't comment but regards the gaze of Maurya in earnest.

The trace of a smile is playing across Maurya's lips now. 'You don't look so good. Do you want some water?'

'No, thank you.'

'Okay. So where was I?' he makes a show of remembering, squeezing one eye shut, 'Oh, yes. That the case is confusing. But not if you turn the case on its head.' He brings his face closer to Sanya. 'There's a great mental model that I learnt from a very wise man. If you're stuck at a problem, unsure of how to solve it, always invert. To know the answer of . . . let's say, how to be happy in life, invert the question. Find out how to be miserable in life and then avoid doing all those things and you'll be happy. How to become rich . . . invert . . . find out how people become poor . . . how to become successful . . . find out how to lose in life—'

'I've got it!' Sanya snaps. 'Please, can you come to the point?'

'Sure,' Maurya chuckles wryly. 'My point is that I inverted this case as well. Instead of speculating on who killed Anant, I addressed the question who could *not* have killed Anant.' He pauses and lets his last statement hang in the air, watching Sanya closely. She looks back without a hint of emotion. 'And I've reached an interesting conclusion.'

Sanya swallows. 'And what might that be?'

'I don't think Mahesh could've killed Anant,' he shakes his head. 'If he's the killer, his schedule that night does not fit with the time of your husband's death. Although his motive was seamless, he was my first elimination. He keeps harping on that he was your husband's friend, but I can't help but think that Mahesh hated your husband's guts, something that you alluded to in your testimony as well.' He pauses to catch his breath and lightly clasps his hand on the table. 'All right, then. So, our second suspect is Vicky. But I've been thinking that it couldn't have been him either. I fail to see any logic whatsoever for his committing the crime . . . Yes, he did have a motive—also, he wasn't very fond of his brother, given that the two brothers barely spoke in the past few months; but the question remains, how did he benefit from his brother's death? He didn't.' He purses his lips and shoots Sanya a piercing glare. 'That leaves you.'

Sanya's heart is hammering in her chest now. She has started shaking.

Maurya goes on, maintaining his icy glare on her, 'I've been able to eliminate those two suspects, but in your case, I'm afraid, I couldn't do it.' Sanya turns her gaze away from Maurya, and he waits until she's looking into his eyes again. 'I think—I think you killed your husband, Mrs Kapoor.' He leans back in his chair, crossing his arms across his chest and pinioning her with a gimlet stare.

Sanya doesn't bother to disguise the fear in her eyes now. Her lips are trembling. Beneath the desk, she has clenched her fists, the nails digging into her palms.

'But the problem in your case is that I couldn't find a motive,' Maurya adds after a long moment. 'You know, intuition is a very strong emotion. I value it more than knowledge and experience in my arsenal, in any sleuth's arsenal, really, although social scientists would argue that intuition is a derivative of experience, and it wouldn't exist without the latter. Be that as it may, I've learnt to trust my instinct. Just an hour ago, I was discussing with my sub-inspector that you might've killed your husband accidentally . . .'

Sanya's face hardens.

'. . . so, tell me Mrs Kapoor, I want to test my instinct here—did you kill your husband accidentally? I hope you won't disappoint me.'

Sanya does not reply for a long moment. The she starts weeping. 'I . . . I'm sorry . . . I'm sorry . . .'

'Please answer the question, Mrs Kapoor.'

Sanya's shoulders start shaking as a fit of sobs seize her. She lowers her head and rests it on the table.

Maurya gives her a minute, clearly put off by . . . the *charade*? Is that it? He isn't sure.

'I am sorry . . .' she mutters, her voice muffled. She sniffles and looks up at Maurya. The mascara has smudged her cheeks. 'I . . . I . . . didn't mean to—'

So, she did kill him? Maurya feels a bolt of electricity course through him. 'Please go on.'

Sanya takes a few shaky breaths and tries to compose herself. She turns to glance at the camera.

'You don't have to look at the camera to confess,' Maurya tells her. 'Just tell us the truth.'

Teary-eyed, she meets Maurya's eyes. 'You're right, inspector . . . but it . . . it was a mistake. I . . . I killed him by accident.' She looks away as another bout of tears overcomes her. She covers her face with both her hands and sobs uncontrollably. Her entire body shakes. After a minute, she rubs her eyes and continues in a low, shaky voice, 'That night he . . . he provoked me. As you already know, we had an argument, and then in the bedroom . . . he pushed me . . . viciously. My head hit the mirror and I had this injury which you saw on the first day,' she indicates the wound on her forehead, 'but that didn't deter him from abusing me further before storming out of our room. I was so heartbroken that I decided I needed a break from him for a few days. Which is why I booked my flight for the next day. But then—'

'But then?' Maurya prompts her.

'I . . . I didn't want to just go without talking it out with him first.' She sniffles again, rubbing her eyes. 'I wanted to ask him why he always did this.'

Maurya's skin prickles. 'Did what?'

Sanya takes a deep breath before answering, 'Um, hitting me, abusing me. I was aware that he had a temper, but why disrespect everyone? A few hours after our fight, I left the bedroom to talk to him in his study in the basement. He was reading a book. His eyes were still red when he glanced up at me from his book. I poured out my heart to him and told him that he cannot keep doing what he does to me. I pleaded with him to give me at least an iota of respect—I was his wife, after all. He started breathing heavily. I could sense that my words had backfired, and I had only ended up infuriating him further. He began yelling, calling me names: "Stupid bitch! You worthless whore! Get out of my house!" He stormed over to me, his right hand raised to hit me. I . . . I stepped back and begged him to . . . to stop . . . but he . . . he hit me again. I tried defending myself and hid my face behind my arms, but he continued pounding his fists on me . . .' Sanya stops talking, her face puckered in a deep frown. She's looking at Maurya, but the inspector senses that she is focusing at some point far away and he just happens to be in the trajectory of her line of sight.

'Mrs Kapoor, are you okay?' There's no response. Her face is expressionless, almost like she's in a trance.

'Mrs Kapoor?' He reaches over and pats her hand a few times. 'Mrs Kapoor . . .'

'Y . . . yes . . .' she squeezes her eyes shut.

'Are you okay?' he asks softy.

Sanya nods quietly, her eyes still shut.

'What happened after that?'

Sanya opens her eyes and Maurya glimpses the pain and fear in them. 'Then . . . then . . . I caught sight of that . . . that vase, and almost instinctively, I . . . I hit him. I'm sorry, I really am sorry . . .' her hands fly to her face, and she croaks in pain. 'I had no intention . . . I lost my self-control . . . it was all too sudden. He . . . he provoked me. After I hit him, his face twisted and he just fell. I was beside him for ten minutes, trying to wake him up . . . but he was dead.'

'What time was this?'

'I went to his study after Mahesh left, so it must've been 11.10 or 11.15.'

'And what did you do after that? I mean after the—'

Sanya groans in anguish. 'I . . . I went up to my room. I didn't know what to do . . . I was so scared . . . I'm sorry . . . sorry . . . it was an accident . . .'

'Hmm.' Maurya scratches the back of his neck. He's elated at finally cracking the case, although his cold and hard expression belies no such emotion. He never thought it would work out the way it did. He just had a hunch about Mrs Kapoor's involvement, but it was just that; he hadn't expected her to crack at the first blow.

He crosses his arms. 'Mrs Kapoor, you mentioned earlier that your husband hit you. It seems like that night wasn't the first time. Can you please tell us how many times he hit you in the past?'

Sanya feels a knot tighten in her stomach. 'A few times.'

Maurya allows himself to smile a little. 'Mrs Kapoor, "a few times" is very vague. Do you have a number—an approximate number will do.'

'About five . . . six times since our marriage.' Then she furrows her brow. 'But why . . . why do you want to know this?'

'Just . . . for our records, that's all. And did he hit you in front of anyone?'

Sanya shakes her head glumly.

Of course, Maurya reflects, *makes sense. Anant wouldn't want to mar his successful-fund-manager image. No one wants to associate with a man who indulged in domestic violence.*

'Did you tell anyone about your husband's violence?'

Sanya shakes her head again. Then, abruptly, she sits up straight in the chair and looks the inspector in the eye, 'Actually, sometimes I discussed it with my helper, Sharda.'

'Oh, is that so?'

'Yes, um, she invariably noticed my injuries, so she—'

'She knew,' Maurya completed the sentence for her, nodding.

'Yes. And then there was this women's welfare organization that I . . . I was visiting—'

'For what?'

Sanya sighs deeply. Maurya can see the fear in her eyes again. 'It was a place for, um, for women who were victims of domestic violence. I wanted to discuss it with someone . . . you know, like get a perspective, hear stories of other women, but at the same time, I . . . I didn't want my problems to come out into the open, so I didn't discuss any of this with my mother or anyone I knew. It would've been so embarrassing for the whole family.'

'Sure. Okay.' Maurya gets to his feet and paces up and down the room, his mind in overdrive. Sanya has lowered her gaze and is studying the floor. Maurya feels a little sorry for the woman, but murder is murder and she will be convicted for it.

He sits down on the chair. 'Mrs Kapoor,' he speaks softly, 'clearly there's a lot you hid from us the first time you narrated your story. Now, I understand you did that to conceal your crime, but I want to hear the complete story. The whole truth, this time.'

Sanya glances up at him. 'I'm sorry that I lied to you before. I . . . I should've come clean the first time, but—' she rubs her eyes with the back of her hands '—I couldn't bring myself to tell the truth. I was so scared.'

Maurya nods. 'I understand.' She isn't the first killer to conceal the truth. He isn't surprised at all. All criminals make an attempt to hoodwink the law and go scot-free. And some do. But not she. She has confessed and her story is over. The case is over. But even so, he is interested to know the entire backdrop of the murder. 'Mrs Kapoor, we would still need to know the full story.

Now that it's all out in the open, please don't hide anything from us, including your husband's behaviour towards you. I assure you I'll do my best to convince the prosecution to grant you a lighter punishment given that the incident took place on the spur of the moment without any premeditation. So please,' he places his hands on the table and laces his fingers, 'tell us everything this time. Hide nothing.'

PART—4

THE CONFESSION

TWENTY-THREE

It wasn't a very happy marriage. Not after the first few months, at least. No marriage can be when there is a lack of understanding and a completely opposite worldview with your partner. I wholeheartedly admit my fault and I am to be equally blamed for all the altercations with Anant. I cannot allow the blame to fall squarely on the head of the only man I've ever loved.

I think Anant was an extremely passionate person, but he could not love anyone more than his work due to his fascination with business and numbers. He was a workaholic and worked sixteen to eighteen hours a day. He barely had any time for the family. But that never bothered me too much. Everybody has the right to live life the way they want to. I've been a free person for most of my life, never tethered to one spot, and I can imagine the disquietude if you have to live life on someone else's terms. I just went along, complaining to Anant, but not too much, for spending very little time with me and let him do what he enjoyed most—investing.

He was a good man, well, most of the time. But sometimes something got into him, and he'd become a completely different person. If I have to be completely honest, I can admit that I never understood him totally. Throughout human history, it has never been easy to understand geniuses after all. Perhaps I should refrain from using the word 'genius' casually, but my husband might have well been one. What else could explain the investing phenomenon that he was, what with the financial media, the journalists and the who's who of the investment community queuing at our door to hobnob with him? Everyone wanted his opinion on the markets and the world economy. Genius or no? Go figure.

If I have to distil my thoughts further, he might have had a multiple-personality disorder. How else can one explain the loving, caring and witty attributes that he harboured most of the time, but on some occasions transmogrified into a pompous, discordant man, pontificating about his glorious achievements while denigrating the mediocrity of others? To an extent, I think, we all have multiple personalities living within ourselves. We're rarely consistent—our thoughts, our desires, opinions and ambitions frequently fluctuate with time. But Anant was an extreme. One moment he'd be smiling and gazing lovingly into your eyes, and the other, he'd be hurling cuss words at you.

It all began a few months after our marriage. The first few months, I admit, were wonderful. We were hopelessly in love and spent our honeymoon for a month in the Maldives. We parasailed, surfed and did the undersea walk; we dined at the best restaurants, ate seafood and drank the finest champagne; we went for long drives in luxurious sedans across the island. Time flew by. That was the only month in our marriage that I had Anant completely to myself. No phone calls, no emails, no market updates. We never had such amazing togetherness again.

Then, a few months later, the first seeds of conflict began arising in our relationship. Anant despised my spending habits. For some inexplicable reason, he didn't want me to spend any money at all. The man was a total miser. He had so much money but barely any desires. Why does a man work at all? To earn money and buy the luxuries life has to offer. Isn't that right? All he did was preach the virtues of compound interest and how the wealthiest people in the world had become rich by compounding their money. His oft-quoted theory was the snowball effect where even small, insignificant amounts of money build upon themselves, becoming larger and larger, when left untouched, like a giant snowball rolling down a hill. And I'd tell him, '*What rubbish*!' What is the point of growing your money when you don't spend it at all?

Okay, fair enough, we had a different worldview when it came to money. However, when I declared I had enough of my own and wouldn't touch his hard-earned money, although he couldn't interfere in my spending habits, I seemed to have inadvertently pricked his manly ego . . . Things quickly went south in our relationship from that point on.

But what really hurt was his occasional chauvinistic behaviour towards me when he got angry. He could never control his temper and the words that emerged from his mouth were molten lava. He'd tell me that I was incapable of doing anything worthwhile in life, having been born with a silver spoon and, worst of all, if he took all my money from me, I'd be left begging on streets, incapable of even feeding myself. Then one day, he remarked that if I were his employee, he would've sacked me ages ago.

However, I learnt to ignore it all because I knew he'd spew all this venom in the heat of the moment, and then, when he cooled down, he'd sit beside me, mortified and deeply remorseful, his arm around my shoulders.

Men are like that, my mother had told me. For a marriage to be long and healthy, a woman must suppress her ego and always keep it a few notches below that of her husband's. It is cringeworthy, but I knew it was true. Despite all the emancipation of the world in general, society will remain patriarchal. Women's equality, feminism are the dreams of a utopian society that doesn't and will never exist. And frankly, I didn't want to rock the boat and challenge the status quo. So, I simply carried on, turning a blind eye to my husband's shortcomings.

However, the problem was more deep-seated than I realized. I like thinking from first principles, and the more I analysed my husband's behaviour, the more I understood where he was coming from. People are essentially different, but Anant never quite understood that. He had preconceived notions about how everyone around him should lead their lives. Any departure from a lifestyle similar to his own should be deprecated. He didn't get that not everyone wants to perch on a swivel chair, on their arse all day long, staring into the white light of a computer screen. Life is meant to be enjoyed, to explore and to satiate our desires, not to toil endlessly and then die one day with a fortune in the bank. It's okay to be different. It isn't okay to categorically reject another person's point of view or foist one's own outlook on life upon them. And that is what I told him every time we had an argument. He'd listen, really try to listen and understand my perspective, but then he would simply fail to get it; either that or perhaps it failed to even register in his stubborn mind.

His brother and I had countless conversations on this very topic. On some occasions, we even discussed this together with Anant but, unfortunately for us, he was very rigid in his view about how the world worked. It never helped; all we did was infuriate him further.

I hid the physical abuse part in my earlier statement because I didn't want to slander my late husband. He was a role model and an inspiration to a lot of people. Indeed, he was wonderful in a lot of ways and despite his shortcomings, I still love him. Love is not a transient emotion. It pains me to even think of the events of that night. But Anant's provocation was so sudden and grave that I lost self-control. He pounded me with his fists in a blind rage and I just reacted in reflex.

That wasn't the first time he had hit me. The first time, as ironical as it may seem, was on the night of our first anniversary. We'd had a minor argument earlier in the evening and, unbeknownst to us, some guests had been eavesdropping. I don't recall the exact reason for our disagreement but almost certainly it had stemmed from something I had splurged on. Both of us had raised our voices. When it occurred to us that we were being watched, we quickly cooled down. After the party Anant broached the topic again in our bedroom, and I asked him to let it be. But he wouldn't stop. One thing led to another, and then he kicked me in my abdomen. I cried out and fell to the floor, clutching my stomach in agony. That satisfied him and he calmed down. The next morning, I will admit, he was extremely apologetic and promised it would never happen again.

But he had so much anger bottled up inside him that he couldn't refrain from hitting me every time our arguments got heated. He hit me a few more times over the last year. It broke my heart each time, but I couldn't discuss it with anyone. Not even with my mother. For one, it was too embarrassing; and two, it wouldn't have helped. Besides, it wasn't he who hit me—as I mentioned earlier, it was this other person within him who would temporarily take over his body. He genuinely seemed to lose control and he was always deeply remorseful after.

But there was someone with whom I did discuss the physical abuse. A few kilometres down the highway, in the outskirts of the city, there is a very old establishment, Charisha Welfare Foundation. I found them on the Internet. They've been around for two decades and are committed to helping and empowering women. Although when I drove in my Mercedes to that place, I wasn't made particularly welcome. However, when I discussed the purpose of my visit, the matron listened to my story compassionately and told me that the number-one affliction for women that the organization was trying to resolve was physical abuse.

She assigned my case to a charming, middle-aged woman, Miss Nath, who listened to my story patiently. Miss Nath gave me a few instructions—mostly to discuss this openly with my husband and explain to him the emotional scars which the abuse caused in our relationship. She also made it clear that, if matters got worse, I should consider reporting it to the authorities. I told her that that wouldn't be necessary, that my husband was a good man, barring his misogyny. She also gave me her phone number and suggested I call her any time I needed to unburden. I visited her a few times whenever Anant and I fought, and she would shake her head in dismay and curse the entire male demographic.

That fateful night, after our argument at the dinner table, I booked a flight ticket to Dehradun to visit my mother simply because I wanted a break. I planned to quietly slip out of the house in the wee hours without informing Anant and not see him for at least a month. What worried me was his intransigence despite all my entreaties. I could no longer handle the physical and emotional abuse. However, leaving my husband high and dry didn't feel right and so, after Mahesh left, I went into the study to inform him of my plans for the following day. I assumed he would be apologetic and contrite, but I was wrong. Clearly his anger had not abated. He looked at me with such fury and loathing in his bloodshot eyes, that I was scared witless.

When he started hitting me, I don't know what went through my mind—perhaps the discussion I had had with Miss Nath about the psychological damage caused by the sustained abuse—and I think what followed next will haunt me forever. I tried to stop him; I screamed and wailed, but he didn't listen. I caught sight of the vase to my right and instinctively reached for it. I don't know how I did what I did, but I had lost all self-control too, and I hit him with it.

I know what I did is unpardonable, and I accept my mistake. I deserve to die like my husband.

TWENTY-FOUR

'Why do women take so much shit lying down? Why can't they stand up to their men?' Kiran is furious when Maurya tells her about Sanya's confession.

Maurya grins. 'I'm sure *you* won't take any shit.' He's pulling open the drawers of his desk, one by one, and rummaging through them.

'What do you mean?' she furrows her brow. 'And what are you looking for?'

'I mean you wouldn't take shit from your husband—assuming you find one.'

'Oh, you can be sure of that. I'll be inflicting all that pain on him, not the other way around.'

Maurya guffaws loudly, his eyes still focused on the items in the drawer. 'I think the chief problem is money—women are too financially dependent on their husbands.'

'But clearly not in this case.'

'Yes,' he nods. 'Not in this case but generally, I mean. Ah . . . got it.' He extracts an inhaler and studies the expiry date printed on it. Satisfied, he slips it into his trousers pocket.

'I've never seen you using that.'

'Yeah, I take it on my mountaineering trips. Oxygen starts depleting as you climb up the mountain.'

'When do you leave?'

'Now—' he looks at his watch. 'Oh, I mean, for my Everest trip, on Monday, but I'm leaving town now.' As he steps away from her, he says, 'Listen, let's just file the charge sheet, no need to probe into that bookie any further; the other team can continue looking into him. As far as I'm concerned, he had nothing to do with the murder. We have the confession. Case closed. Goodbye.'

'Have a good trip,' Kiran calls out, but Maurya has already trotted out of the door with a spring in his step.

The next morning, Maurya is in an upbeat mood. He has managed to solve the case just before leaving for his two-week-long trip with his buddies from school. He'll be meeting them at the airport the following evening and flying to Kathmandu. From there, they will trek to the Everest base camp.

Almost twelve months without a break. Phew!

He lives in a two-bedroom apartment in the Gurgaon police colony in the southeast district. The apartment is sparsely furnished, befitting a bachelor. Inside the bedroom he is cheerfully packing his clothes, mostly woollens, in a big duffel bag and humming an old song. Sunlight pours in through the window behind the bed.

Although he hates it, the case and the conversations that he had with the people involved keep playing at the back of his head. He always does a thorough post-analysis of all his cases to learn from his mistakes, to analyse what he missed, what tipped him off, understand the psychology of the criminal and so on. It helps sharpen his deductive skills.

However, he doesn't want to do this exercise now. Not when he is off duty and planning a holiday. But the thoughts don't cease. Particularly those with Mahesh and Vicky as they are innocent. He keeps thinking about how close he had got to convicting Mahesh.

At one point, Maurya had been absolutely certain that Mahesh was the killer. He hated Anant, had a motive, had slipped into the house through the back door the second time, had lied about it and, the best part, had a ready alibi. Anyone with even the most basic deductive skills would suspect him. But he wasn't the killer. It was just bad timing that he was at the crime scene a few minutes before the murder. And his apparent motive threw them off track for some time. Luckily Sanya confessed, or he would be still under suspicion.

And Vicky? A total nitwit. The mutual antagonism between the brothers over the last few months, his urgent requirement for a large sum of money to fulfil his obligation to the bookie made him a suspect. That, along with his weak alibi. But, clearly, he had nothing to do with the murder. He was just a burden on his brother and the family. With his brother dead and sister-in-law behind bars, he'll have a good time now. And the money? Who gets it now?

He is pulling out a jacket from the cupboard when he stops abruptly. His heart begins to beat faster. He throws the jacket on top of the bag and sits down on the bed with a thump. A thousand needles prickle at the back of his neck. He tries to recall his conversations with Vicky and Sanya with mounting unease.

Something is not right.

He gets up and starts to pace back and forth in the small living room, his anxiety deepening with every passing minute. A deep foreboding gnaws at his heart that he might have missed something crucial. He recaps all the conversations he has had with the three suspects over the past week. In hindsight, they all point to a theory which he hadn't thought of earlier; something in clear sight all along. *But could it be possible?*

He rushes back to the bedroom and picks up his phone from the bed. He scrolls down to Kiran's number.

'Hey, listen, I want you to do a couple of things for me.' After setting out a few tasks for Kiran, he hesitates, taking a deep breath, and then adds, 'and hold on to that charge sheet for a while, please.'

When Kiran hangs up, she stares at her phone in surprise. *Does he want to pursue this case further?* She wrinkles her forehead in confusion and sets off to carry out the tasks she had been assigned.

TWENTY-FIVE

By afternoon, they have a list of half a dozen people whom Maurya plans to interview. They were guests at the party one year ago at Sanya and Anant's wedding anniversary, mostly relatives, although distant.

But before that, Anant decides to pay a visit to Charisha Welfare Foundation. After driving for a few kilometres straight down the Delhi–Gurgaon Expressway, Maurya takes the last exit. He follows the directions on his phone's GPS and takes a few turns to find himself on a dirt road leading to seemingly nowhere. The foundation is at the end of the road, to the left. There's a huge iron gate at the entrance. Maurya parks his jeep outside it and alights.

He is soon standing in front of an old, decrepit, red-brick building in the middle of nowhere. There are open fields on both sides and a few makeshift shops towards the left. He enters the building and heads for the reception.

The old lady behind the counter greets him with a smile. Maurya introduces himself and explains the purpose of his visit to her.

'Sanya Kapoor,' she says, smiling genially. 'Yes, yes. I remember her.' She removes her glasses and puts them on the desk in front of her. 'Wonderful child. She was very friendly around here. All the volunteers loved her. Extremely generous girl. She'd bring us all gifts whenever she visited.'

'I think Miss Nath was handling her case?'

'Yes, yes, indeed, it was Miss Nath. She handles most of the physical abuse cases.' Then a frown appears on her face. 'Poor girl. Her husband hits her. God should punish that man.'

So, she doesn't know. Maurya debates whether he should tell her that God had indeed punished the man but decides against it. 'Can I speak to Miss Nath, please?'

'Sure.' She gets up slowly and disappears into the nether regions of the building. She returns a minute later, accompanied by another middle-aged woman.

Miss Nath greets Maurya amiably and leads him down the hallway to a bench overlooking the lawn in front.

'Yes,' she says, sitting down. 'What do you want to know about Sanya?'

After taking a seat, Maurya clears his throat and decides to tell her everything. She gasps. 'Did Sanya kill her husband?'

Maurya nods.

'I don't believe it!'

'But she has confessed to us.'

Miss Nath stares at the inspector in disbelief. 'But she was such a kind and good-natured woman. How could she—'

'She didn't intend to,' Maurya shakes his head. 'It was a mistake. A spur-of-the-moment crime.'

Miss Nath's eyes are wide behind her glasses as she looks in surprise at the inspector, 'But if she has already confessed, why are you here?'

Maurya replies after a beat, 'Background check.' He licks his lips. 'Um, could you please tell me how many times she visited this place?'

Miss Nath heaves a deep sigh. 'I think I can count the number of times on my fingers. Four or five times, perhaps.'

'And did she mention anything about the brother? Her husband's brother, I mean.'

'Yes,' Miss Nath nods. 'She always told me that her husband treated his brother just as shabbily as he treated her. From what I understand, her husband had major anger-management issues. He couldn't stop himself once he got going, you know. His arms and legs would flail in all directions. Crazy guy.'

'Yes, I've been told that,' Maurya states, scratching his chin. 'And, um, when did she visit you last?'

Miss Nath narrows her eyes. 'I think . . . erm . . . about two months ago. Her husband had punched her in the abdomen, and Sanya,' she winces, scrunching up her nose, 'had this deep, red bruise. Must have hurt the poor girl badly.'

'But why did she never complain to the police?'

'Oh, I told her that, but . . . I think she was torn between loving her husband and hating him. She'd tell me that she didn't want to malign her husband publicly; he was a finance guy, I think, and very popular among his brethren.'

Maurya sits there for a few minutes, wondering whether he should ask a few more questions. He isn't particularly satisfied with the answers he had managed to get. *Still*, he thinks, *this was worth the visit*.

'Thank you, Miss Nath,' he says as he leaves.

The next morning, DCP Sandhu grimaces at Maurya as he steps in the station.

'We need to talk. My room,' he says and pivots on his heel.

Maurya feels the muscles in his face tighten.

'What's this, Maurya?' the DCP barks as soon as they both sit down across from each other. 'Why aren't you filing the charge sheet?' He crosses his arms and gives a faint snort. 'I thought you already had a confession.'

'Yes, but—'

'What?'

'I . . . I just need a day or two more. There could be more to this than meets the eye—'

'Oh, come on, Maurya, you have the confession. What else do you need?' Sandhu was glaring at him now. 'Anyway, aren't you supposed to be on leave now?'

'Yes, I am!' Maurya shoots back. 'So, you can understand, I wouldn't do what I'm doing if it weren't important.'

Sandhu leans forward in his chair. 'But how do you explain this, Maurya? First you arrest her, then you release her and then when you have her confession, yet you're not pressing charges?' He throws out his arms helplessly. 'I'm at a loss to understand this. Do you think there's someone else involved?'

'I am—I'm not 100 per cent sure, sir,' Maurya replies. 'Like I said, please give me a day or two.'

The frown eases on Sandhu's face, although he still appears unconvinced. 'And what about your leave?'

'I can go afterwards. Getting to the bottom of this murder mystery is much more important now.' He looks at Sandhu anxiously, 'Please don't assign the case to someone else. I'll close it soon.'

'You'd better,' orders Sandhu. 'You'd better.'

TWENTY-SIX

Over the rest of the morning and the afternoon, Maurya interviews the relatives of the Kapoor family who attended the couple's first anniversary—not just those from within the city, but also the rest from the whole of the national capital region.

Late that evening, he sits behind his desk at the station in a foul mood and glances at the wall clock. It's time for him to leave for the airport for his trip. *Damn*! But he is only partially satisfied with some of the answers he's got. Not conclusive, but at least they seem to point in the same direction as his new theory.

He rewinds the conversations in his head one more time, to be sure that he hasn't missed anything relevant.

'Please tell me your name and how you are related to the deceased.'

'My name is Harsh. I'm Anant and Vicky's cousin. I haven't spoken to them for quite some time now as I shifted to Mumbai. I'm just visiting the city for a business meeting and I'll leave tomorrow.'

'Weren't you present at Anant and Sanya's first wedding anniversary?'

'Oh yes, indeed. It was a massive gathering at their place and a lot of people were invited.'

'What was the relationship between the two brothers like?'

'Like Lord Ram and Lakshman, really. Vicky was extremely respectful of his brother, fearful as well. His brother's wish was his command. I've never seen him disobeying his elder brother. And Anant was extremely fond of his little brother and pampered him a lot.'

'But what happened in the last few months of Anant's life? The brothers were not even on speaking terms.'

'That surprises me. Vicky never had the audacity to go against his brother's wishes.'

'So how do you explain the gambling? Although his brother never approved of it, he continued to lose tons of money.'

'The allure of easy money always fascinated Vicky, yes. And Anant always turned a blind eye to it. He never put any pressure on his brother. In fact, Anant often told him that he earned enough for both of them put together, and his little brother could take it easy and enjoy life.'

'Really? I thought Anant hated his gambling addiction and had stopped helping him financially.'

'Yes, that happened later. That is something that surprises me. Perhaps Vicky went overboard with his gambling and lost a fortune. That might have irked Anant. Nevertheless, the two brothers not being on talking terms bewilders me.'

'And what about Mrs Kapoor? How well do you know her?'

'That day was the first and last time I met her.'

'I heard that the couple had a fight that day. Were you a witness to the argument?'

'No, not me. But my mom saw them.'

'Oh . . . okay. Then I would like to see her as well. But before I let you go, how were the brothers that day?'

'Same. The loving brothers I've always known. All the cousins got together after a long time and we had a blast that day. Both brothers were sozzled. I didn't sense any animosity between them.'

'Thank you.'

'Yes, I'm Nirmala, Harsh's mother and sister of Anant's father.'

'Harsh mentioned that you witnessed the argument between Anant and Sanya on the day of their anniversary. Can you throw some light on it? What was it about?'

'Yes, of course. I was going into the house to use the washroom when I heard them shouting at each other. I was surprised, given that it was their anniversary. They didn't see me until I was on my way out, and then, they just stopped abruptly when they caught sight of me. But then, a moment later, Anant brushed me aside and continued screaming at Sanya. I found that really odd. The poor girl must have been deeply embarrassed by my presence.'

'Would you be able to recall what—'

'Yes, yes. I remember some of it. Anant was insulting Sanya, his tone was very harsh. Sanya had also raised her voice, but hers was nowhere near as loud as Anant's. Sanya was begging him to stop. I think she had bought a fancy car for herself and Anant didn't approve of it, or something like that. He was furiously admonishing her for her extravagance.'

'Was there anyone else who witnessed this?'

'Yes, um, there were few other people, and then eventually Vicky intervened and all of us dispersed.'

'You remember these other witnesses?'

'Um . . . I think there was Satish, our cousin. He lives in Delhi.'

'Anyone else?'

'There were a few others whom I didn't recognize. It was a big gathering, you see . . . er, wait a minute, I think there was my brother's daughter, Neha, as well who saw them arguing.'

'Okay, thanks. And would you agree with your son that Anant and Vicky had a very cordial relationship throughout their life?'

'Oh, absolutely! We would often cite their affection as an example to our children.'

'But then what changed towards the end?'

'I have no idea. People change, I guess.'

'Thank you.'

'Mr Satish, we met your sister, Nirmala, and she told us that—'

'Yes, I'm aware. She called me. But why are you interested in knowing what happened a year ago? How does it have any bearing on your case?'

'We're just making sure that there we aren't missing anything. Now, can you tell me what happened that day between Anant and Mrs Kapoor? Why were they fighting?'

'I think my sister told you everything, didn't she? I too was surprised to find them arguing—Anant was hollering at the top of his voice—and even though there were so many onlookers, it didn't deter him. I had never seen Anant in such a rage before.'

'Didn't you try to intervene?'

'Oh, I did, but he wouldn't listen. He said something like, "She keeps throwing my money on stuff we don't need and one day, we'll have to sell something that we do need." He was very agitated. I tried to calm him down, but he stopped yelling only when Vicky arrived. There were a lot of guests hovering around and that might have embarrassed the family.'

'And what did Vicky do?'

'He pacified the couple. He whispered something to them and led them into the house. They emerged after a while, clearly pretending that everything was normal.'

'I see. Can you also tell me how the brothers were behaving that day?'

'Normal. They were good with each other.'

'That is something I'm unable to wrap my head around. If the brothers were so friendly and respectful to each other, what happened towards the end? Why did they begin hating each other?'

'They did? Really? I'm not aware of that.'

'Yes, they hadn't been speaking to each other for months.'

'Is that right? I'm clueless. I find that very odd.'

'Thank you for your time.'

'I'm Neha, second cousin to Vicky and . . . erm . . . Anant.'

'I really hope you can help me. D'you have any idea what changed between the brothers in the past one year? Everyone says that they were the best of brothers, caring and loving, but then what happened towards the end? Why wouldn't they even talk to each other?'

'I think it was because of Vicky's gambling addiction. He lost a lot of money and—'

'But Anant had lot of money! He was all over on the financial media. I can understand Vicky's gambling addiction might have angered him, but Anant almost disowned his brother.'

'Not really.'

'A bookie threatened Vicky's life for two crore rupees. Surely, that is a mere drop in the bucket for Anant. So, what happened? Why did he not help his beloved brother?'

'I can't say I know the answer to that, but I'm guessing he was very angry due to all the gambling—'

'I don't think so. I understand the anger part, but Anant would surely do everything in his power to protect his brother if he really was the loving, responsible brother everyone claims he was. Or is everyone lying?'

'No, they're right. Anant was a great elder brother. I wish I had a brother like that.'

'Thank you for your help, although I didn't really get the answer.'

Kiran sits down across from Maurya. She looks over her shoulder at the time. 7.10 p.m. Maurya doesn't even notice her presence and his face is twisted in a grimace, his brow knitted in confusion.

'What's happened, boss?' Kiran gives him a wry smile. 'You should be at the airport now.'

Maurya smiles thinly. 'I can't go until I get to the bottom of this.'

'But I don't see what else is left. The killer has confessed.'

Maurya looks at her, shaking his head in disappointment. Kiran holds his gaze, puzzled. 'You're not able to see it, Kiran. There is something else happening here.'

'See what?'

'Okay, think.' He leans forward, throwing her a hard glare. 'I understand Vicky had a gambling addiction, but if Anant was the kind of brother that everyone says he was, and with the money he had, why did he just throw his brother under the bus? I mean, almost literally. The bookie threatened to chop off Vicky's legs, and Anant didn't turn a hair. What do you think Anant's net worth is? And how much percentage do you think two crores would be of his net worth? I'm sure that it'll be insignificant. That bungalow alone would be over thirty crores.'

'I can find that out. I'll look through his financials.'

'Yes, do that. He was an extremely wealthy man, so why couldn't he part with a small amount to save his brother?'

'And his wife is equally wealthy. The entire family's wealth would be—'

'Yes, yes,' Maurya nods. 'While you're at it, look at both their accounts. I find it very odd that Anant didn't help his brother. And what happened to cause the rift between the brothers just a few months before Anant's death?'

'Only one person can answer that.'

Maurya glances at his watch. *Not that late*. 'Call him in right now for questioning.'

PART—5

VICKY KAPOOR'S STORY

TWENTY-SEVEN

I always held my brother in high esteem. Our parents passed away when I was fifteen years old and ever since, it was always my brother to whom I turned for help for every challenge that life threw at me. He was ten years older than me, but there was a generation gap between us in terms of the responsibilities that he shouldered; I was just a kid for him and he always tried to protect me. He'd address me as 'kiddo'.

Ironically, it was because of him and the security his presence provided that I developed my lackadaisical attitude towards life, an attribute that he despised. A week has passed since his death, and the more I think about him, the more I realize that because of his towering presence in my life, I could do as I pleased and live life on my terms, never concerned about the repercussions. He was like the sails of a powerless ship, always guiding me to safer waters.

It is true that I'm addicted to gambling, a vice that I picked up in the company of my school friends. My brother always warned me that the path of easy money always turns out to be harder in the long run. Short-term gain inevitably leads to long-term pain. But I paid him no heed. In the initial days, I wagered insignificant amounts of money, but as beginner's luck favoured me, I never even realized when the stakes went up, so much so that it spiralled out of control. To compensate my losses I had to wager even more, and I soon found myself plunging into a self-created abyss of despair.

Luckily, I had my sister-in-law who always guided me and has been extremely supportive. I'm not scared of Sanya like I was of my brother, and I would discuss a lot of issues with her that I didn't have the courage to talk about with Anant. She was a very good listener and always offered solutions. For instance, the first time I discussed a big loss with her, she was very calm about it. She didn't judge me, unlike my brother who'd always criticize my frivolity, despite all the good intentions he might have had.

I walked into her room sometime in winter last year when she was reading a book. Anant was out of town on a business trip. I had lost a significant amount of money that day, my largest until that point, and I needed a patient person to hear me out without condemning me.

'Look at your face, Vicky. All red and sour,' she teased me with a smile. 'How much did you lose today?'

I sat on the chair by her bed. 'My entire month's pocket money.'

'Pocket money!' she snorted. 'It's your money, after all, even though your brother gives it to you.'

'Yes, I know, but—'

She turned to face me, sitting cross-legged on the bed. 'Okay, listen up. My father taught me a few tricks about gambling. All his life he did just that, but the difference is that he gambled in the stock market. The key difference between a winner and a loser in the long term is not that a winner never loses. No.' She shook her head. 'He loses all the time; it's a game of odds after all. Probabilities will always work against you some of the time. The trick is to always win big when you're right and lose small, or fold your bet when you're wrong. Keep doing that and the math of large numbers will eventually favour you.'

I had already started to feel better by then. This is what she always did—provided solutions without preaching sermons and taking jabs at me. 'I think what you're saying makes sense.'

'Whatever I say always makes sense, kiddo!' she giggled, winking at me, sort of mimicking Anant. That was his usual statement. 'And listen, no matter what your brother says, I do not condemn your gambling, provided that you can do it intelligently. If that is your passion you should follow it, but be diligent about it. Always plan your moves and get the odds on your money like a casino. Only then, bet big.'

'Thank you so much, Sanya. You're the best.'

'I know, although your brother thinks he's the best and everyone around him is dumb.'

'Grrrr.' I made a dismissive gesture with my hand. 'His being smart does not make other people stupid. You're equally smart. And you know that.'

Her eyes glittered behind her glasses and she smiled, eyes crinkling at the corners. 'Thank you.'

I wondered whether she too needed a pep talk every now and then, just like I did. Anant was a good man, but he was not the easiest man to be married to. He had his idiosyncrasies. Despite being as rich as Croesus, he always criticized Sanya at even the least sign of extravagance. He always wanted to keep a track of all, no matter how tiny, expenses. My brother was a skinflint, there was no question about that. But what I truly disliked about him was that he'd castigate her in public. On their first wedding anniversary he lambasted her in front of guests, without an iota of courtesy or respect for her. I had to intervene and stop him otherwise he'd have carried on with his rant, causing her no end of embarrassment. Later that night, in their bedroom, he hit her. Sanya told me about it the next morning. Naturally, he wouldn't hit her when I was around.

'No, really, it's true,' I said. 'I know he thinks very highly of himself.'

'And because of that he wants us to live life on his terms.'

'But that isn't right! He can do as he pleases, but he cannot dictate our lives!'

Her face hardened. 'But that's exactly what he does, doesn't he? I can't buy what I want to buy. You can't do something that you love doing because your brother doesn't like it. You need his permission for everything.'

I exhaled sharply. It was true. My brother really controlled our lives. I had nothing of my own and depended on Anant for everything—even our father's money that should've ideally been split in half. Anant had taken my share and invested it all in his business, promising me that he would grow it multi-fold. But the problem is that I still had to ask him to give me 'my' money. And then I had to explain to him what I needed it for. I couldn't say gambling, even though I was sure that my destiny would turn around sooner than later with a big win. I just needed one huge killing to cover all my losses. Of course I couldn't tell him that.

Sanya was right. We were too dependent on my brother.

'But there's nothing we can do, right?' I asked in a low voice. 'He's the boss.'

Sanya nodded. 'Yes, you're right.' She removed her glasses and placed them on the bedside table. Then she scooched forward to sit on the edge of the bed, her feet touching the floor. 'But you shouldn't be afraid of him. You shouldn't hesitate to tell him that it's your money that you ask for, and whatever you use it for is your prerogative. Don't you think?'

'Yes, you're right,' I replied brightly. It was refreshing to know that someone else's thoughts resonated with what I'd been feeling for some time now.

'Okay, go now,' she said. 'I have to sleep. And remember to stand up for yourself.'

I left the room still wondering why my brother felt the need to control my life so much.

Over the next few weeks I did try to stand up for myself as Sanya had suggested, but it didn't really help. Anant never wanted anyone else's opinion; he just wanted to bulldoze everyone around him. Unfortunately, I wasn't able to win big in any of my bets, and I had to eventually go back to my brother. He'd give it, dour-faced, making sure to rub my ineptitude in my face.

Why don't you get a real job?

Can you stop being a punter and become serious with your life?

I can't just keep giving you money only for you to lose it all!

How did you become like this? Look at me and look at yourself! You don't deserve to be my brother!

The more I retaliated and complained, the more it aggravated him. I loved him, but the man dug his heels in when it came to his money. If I broached the topic of my inheritance, all hell would break loose. After giving me a severe tongue-lashing, he'd throw me out of the room.

I thought that was unfair. All of it. He had no right to tell me what to do with my life. My share of the inheritance is enough to last me my whole life, so why did I need his permission? I am very passionate about the art of gambling and the law of numbers. The returns are very asymmetrical. Many people spend their lives slogging all day in an office and, despite that, most of them don't have enough for their retirement. I'd much rather die than lead such a mundane, colourless life.

In a way, Sanya and I share the exact same outlook on life. Both of us are free spirits who like taking life easy, living each day as it comes. Our opinion on Anant has always converged. We discussed him a lot and Sanya always encouraged me and boosted my morale whenever I fell out with Anant.

Over the last few months, I had started speaking my mind to Anant and it almost always ended in a bitter altercation. Sometimes Sanya would intervene and support me, but Anant would invariably tell her to stay out of his family matters. *Really?* It was insane. We were all one family.

Sanya and I would discuss for hours on how to make Anant understand that we were different people and to let us be. It was getting very difficult to even talk to him, let alone make him understand anything. His ideology was so deep-rooted that no other opinion made sense to him. It was always about working hard, earning money, spending less than you earned and investing the rest to compound your money. But when you had so much money, what was the need to save more? Why not indulge a little?

During summer this year, I couldn't resist the urge to tell my brother everything that I thought of him. Until then, I had held back and been very subtle and low-key during our arguments, invariably acquiescing in the end. But not any more. I'd had a very long discussion with Sanya, and she had put together a comprehensive and convincing argument for me to put forth to my brother. She insisted that I demand to have my share of the inheritance, along with the interest earned, and deposit the money in my bank account, so that I didn't ever have to ask my brother for money again. Thanks to Sanya, who had always given me sane advice, I clawed back control of my life from Anant's clutches. She has been a lovely sister-in-law.

That day, the conversation with Anant quickly turned heated, and I did not restrain myself from raising my voice. I hollered back at him and told him that he needed to return my money that very day otherwise I would have to call a lawyer to intervene. Sanya had shared the contact details of her lawyer friend who specialized in family disputes.

'What the hell is wrong with you?' Anant was glowering at me. 'How dare you threaten me with legal proceedings? Do whatever you have to! I'd much rather turn your money over to a charity than give it to you and watch you blow it up as you've always done!'

As always he won the argument, and honestly, I didn't have the guts to call the lawyer and go against him publicly.

We stopped talking to each other from that day. Whenever I needed money, I'd ask Sanya. She has been very supportive, and not once did she turn down my request. Perhaps she was giving me her own money.

But then I screwed up one day. Inebriated, I placed a very large bet in the hope of making a fortune. I lost a huge sum. Two crores. But the worst part was that I was now indebted to a notoriously nasty bookie. My friend had advised me to keep the bet small because I couldn't afford to default against this particular bookie, but the frustration of always having to beg for money was getting to me, so I took a chance and lost.

Just a few days before he passed away, I had spoken to Anant after months and made a clean breast of it about the bet. Although I asked Sanya for help, she couldn't conjure up such a huge amount in a short time, and she asked me to tell Anant everything. She was sure he would help. But he didn't. I couldn't believe it. How could my brother turn his back on me like that? He was a such a loving brother. Did he think that I was lying? I'm not sure.

The bookie's men had given me a deadline of ten days. On the night of Anant's death, I went to meet a friend and discuss my options. I was terrified. Sanya called me and once again told me to try and convince Anant; there was no other option. She asked me to call him that very day, and no matter what, persuade him to give me the money.

After bidding my friend goodbye, I left the bar and called Anant from my car. Once again, I pleaded with him. I assured him that I was speaking the truth about the dangerous bookie and that I really needed the money.

But he adamantly refused to believe me. I almost threw my phone out. I was that angry.

I went straight to bed after coming home that night, planning to have a physical fight with him the next morning. If I had to hit him to get the money, so be it.

But he was already dead by then.

TWENTY-EIGHT

'By the time Vicky was almost at the end of his statement, I was fairly sure he would admit to killing his brother, or at least confess that he had partnered with his sister-in-law to kill him.'

Maurya nods but doesn't reply. He is sipping his tea slowly.

Outside it has become dark and most of the staff, except the night-duty patrol, have left the station. Kiran has decided to stay a little while longer because she is now convinced that Maurya is right. There is much more to the case.

'It's difficult to see through the maze,' Maurya glances at Kiran. 'Do you have all the information that I asked for?'

'Yes.'

'Good,' He gets to his feet and throws the plastic coffee cup in the bin beside his desk. 'Let's meet tomorrow and get this over with.'

The next morning, instead of heading to the station, Maurya drives to south Delhi. Kiran has collated all the information they have on Sanya. They're first going to visit her college in Munirka, from where she graduated almost a decade ago. Kiran had done some homework by telephoning the college beforehand and finding out whether there was a teacher who remembered Sanya. Luckily for them, there was a Mrs Nadgir who had been teaching international law in that college for two decades and risen to the rank of vice principal. She had taken few minutes and had put Kiran's call on hold, before confirming that she did recall Sanya.

Now, Maurya and Kiran are seated in her small office, across from her.

Mrs Nadgir is a short, stout woman in her mid-fifties. She is smiling politely at her guests. 'I did see it in the news. Did Sanya really kill her husband?'

Maurya clears his throat and ignores her question. 'Can you please tell us what sort of a person Sanya was? Anything you remember will help us.'

Mrs Nadgir frowns at Maurya's brusqueness. She purses her lips and thinks for a minute or two. 'I think, um, she was a good kid. I remember she was not the brightest in class, but she always managed to do well in the exams. She was a good-natured, cheerful person. I quite liked her which is why I'm not sure that she could've—'

'Is there anything else you remember?'

Mrs Nadgir eyes the inspector scornfully. 'What do you really want to know?'

Maurya glances at Kiran before asking, 'I mean, was she a violent person? Did she have any fights when she was here?'

'Violent?' Mrs Nadgir shakes her head. 'Not at all. In fact, she was very friendly with most of the kids. She was the kind of person who would stand up for her friends.'

'Can you please elaborate?'

'It was a long time ago, um, I don't remember when exactly. I think there was a girl who had got pregnant with a boy from her class. If I recall correctly, Sanya was in the same class and she was a friend, or at least the two girls knew each other well. This boy was, um, a brash kid who refused to have anything to do with this girl after impregnating her. I don't know what happens to kids in their twenties, they become so impulsive. This girl slashed her wrists in despair. She survived, but Sanya and a few other girls brewed up a storm in college, demanding the rustication of this boy with immediate effect. These girls were so adamant and obdurate, and even threatened a hunger strike if we didn't meet their demands. The college was also getting a lot of negative media attention, and the college management eventually got rid of that boy.'

Maurya nods his head slowly. 'But do you know whether Sanya was leading this protest or was it some other girl?'

'I don't know that. Sorry.'

'Is there anything else you recall? Something specific. Particularly related to Sanya.'

Mrs Nadgir looks down at the desk and tries to recall. Maurya is staring at her intently. After a few moments, she looks up and says in a tone of finality, 'I'm sure I don't remember anything specific other than Sanya being a sweet, friendly kid.'

Maurya sighs. 'Thank you for your time.'

Next, they proceed to Anand and Associates, the law firm in Delhi where Sanya had worked for a few weeks. Maurya doesn't expect to gather significant information from here, but he wants to understand why Sanya left the firm so soon.

The office is in the bustling Kamla Nagar Market in north Delhi, on the first floor of a commercial building. Maurya and Kiran take the stairs and enter the first room to their left. The receptionist leads them to the cabin of Mr Anand at the far end of the office.

Mr Anand is a middle-aged man with silver-white hair and a rotund face. He gets up when the two police officers enter his cabin, respectfully offers them chairs across his desk and sits down after his guests have settled down.

'How can I help you, sir?'

'I want to know about Sanya Kapoor,' Maurya starts without preamble. 'She was working here, wasn't she?'

'Sanya Kapoor?' Confusion spreads across Mr Anand's face. 'Hardly. She was here for barely a month, if I recall correctly.'

'Yes, yes. That is what I want to know. What was the reason behind it?'

'Reason behind her quitting, you mean?'

Maurya nods.

'The answer might sound stupid, but she left because she didn't want to work around so many men.'

Maurya and Kiran exchange glances. 'Around men?' Kiran asks, puzzled. 'What exactly do you mean?'

'She was a weird woman,' Mr Anand replies, scratching his nose. 'She would demand silly explanations from me about why were there no women in the office. I asked her how that mattered. We hire people based on their skills. For instance, I told her that we had hired her despite her being a woman. There is no gender disparity here.'

'And then?' Maurya asks.

'That's it,' Mr Anand snaps his fingers. 'She hated taking orders from the other guys around here. One fine day, she walked into my cabin and literally threw her resignation papers in my face.'

Kiran shakes her head, trying to make sense of all this and wondering if it was helping the case. In her peripheral vision, she notices a grim expression on Maurya's face. Just then her phone rings, and she steps out of the office to answer the call due to the poor signal reception inside.

A few minutes later, Maurya is done with further questioning and walks thoughtfully to his jeep, where Kiran is patiently waiting for him.

'You won't believe this,' she announces as soon as Maurya is within earshot, 'but I have some baffling information about the financial status of the Kapoor family that'll knock your socks off.'

PART—6

CONCLUSION

TWENTY-NINE

'Hello, Mrs Kapoor. So nice to see you again. I hope you are well and the guards are treating you well.'

Sanya's ears prick up with pleasure at the warm welcome. She sits down. When the guard closes the interrogation room's door behind her, she replies, 'Yes, I'm fine, thank you. What brings you here? Do you have more questions? When does my trial start?'

Maurya laughs, waving his hand dismissively. 'Don't worry about that. We've enough time for all that. Let's have a nice conversation first. I think I'm beginning to understand you better now.'

'What do you mean?'

'You know, Kiran and I, right from the beginning, dismissed you as a foolish woman. The first time when we arrested you, we wondered how you could have been so stupid as to leave your fingerprints on the murder weapon and not even attempt to establish an alibi. Every murderer does that. That is murder 101. But then, unfortunately, the other two suspects also had motives and weak alibis. It would have got very difficult to convict you in court as the defence counsel would have dismissed our theory out of hand. And so, lo and behold, we had to release you. Not only that. All of us truly believed that you couldn't have killed your husband.

'But, if you didn't kill your husband, who did? Anant certainly didn't commit suicide and there was no evidence of an attempted burglary gone awry—we had sufficient proof of that. So, my suspicion then fell on Mahesh. His timing was perfect. He left the house just a few minutes before the murder. And the best part, he had an alibi all ready and that made me extremely suspicious. Did you know that he entered the house a second time through the back door, and he didn't tell me about it the first time we questioned him? Of course, he became our suspect. Add to it the fact that he wasn't particularly fond of your husband, which you mentioned as well.

'Everything fitted perfectly. I was convinced that Mahesh was the killer. But then, an almost negligible observation, at least at first, made me change my mind. When I first saw the corpse of your husband, I noticed the gash was on the left side of his forehead. Instinctively, it struck me that the killer had to be right-handed, but Mahesh is a leftie. I didn't arrive at this theory until after having a few conversations with Mahesh. What struck me as odd was how Mahesh could kill Anant and then rush to his friend's bungalow within the next ten minutes with all his emotions under perfect control. He isn't a cold-blooded murderer, right?

'I do think, however, that Mahesh has been lying to us all along that that night was the first time that he requested your husband to collaborate again. He didn't want us to know it, but it is clear to me that he badly needed your husband to save his firm. But why did he lie? I'm guessing he wanted to save himself from public embarrassment and salvage his reputation. Who would give him any money to invest if it became public knowledge that Mahesh is not a capable investor and is dependent on his partner? Putting my suspicion of him on the backburner, although always doubting my own theory, I moved on to the next suspect.

'Your brother-in-law, Vicky. He had an alibi, but again, weak. He had a motive—he badly needed the money. And what really made me suspicious about him was that he wasn't very fond of his brother. In fact, the brothers didn't even speak to each other for months. But what I could not understand is how killing his brother would help him at all. He still didn't get the money. In fact, all of Anant's money will flow to you as per the Hindu Succession Act. And that made me curious. He may have hated his brother, but he couldn't have killed him. At least the odds were low.

'And that brought me back to you. I was not sure that you killed your husband; I had just eliminated the other two suspects, but not with a lot of conviction. It was possible that they could have still killed Anant. But then, luckily for me, you confessed. I honestly never expected it. I had barely started putting pressure on you when you caved. Just perfect. Case closed.

'But then, when I was home and not even thinking about the case, your statement kept echoing in my ears. I couldn't understand what it was, but something kept nagging at me. Your choice of words, particularly. You kept saying that on the night of the murder, your husband "provoked" you and that you "lost your self-control". You also said that your husband's provocation was "sudden and grave". And that the murder was "a mistake, an accident". Fair enough. It all made sense. But when these words kept running through my head repeatedly and I sensed that something wasn't right.

'I'm guessing that, by now, you've already guessed what I'm driving at. You also mentioned in your statement that you worked in a law firm for just a few weeks. You know, only this morning, I visited your law firm. Nice, friendly Mr Anand said that he never quite understood you; he found you weird. But there was another thing he told me. That you were very good at law. Specifically, criminal law. You remembered all the sections of all the codes by heart. He was equally surprised when I told him that you never took up another job. He was baffled. His words: "Such a smart, clever woman would've made a brilliant criminal lawyer; her opponents would've been fearful of her."

'I think I know what happened. You found Anant. He was rich, famous and, luckily for you, your family friend.

You weren't honest in both your statements. You told us that he wanted to marry you, but I think *you* wanted to marry him. For the money. And do you know why you wanted the money so badly? It was because you had none of your own. I repeat. Nothing. Your father lost it all. Sure, he was a successful stockbroker, you were right about that, but what you conveniently forgot to tell us was that he lost it all by making a few reckless bets. We checked all his bank accounts, Demat accounts and all his other holdings. He had nothing left. He died of a heart attack, yes, but it was due to anxiety and depression of having lost his fortune.

'You've been lying to us all along. You have no money of your own. You were truly dependent on Anant's money. To add to your misery, you've been a reckless spendthrift all your life. Your father didn't care because he had lot of money in his hey days and you were his daughter, his "precious angel". But your husband, despite having far more money than your father ever had, turned out to be a miser and so much wiser. He outright disapproved of your extravagant spending habits and you hated that.

'But I know what you hated more about him. That he was a chauvinist. I accept that he held you in contempt and demeaned you in front of other people, but do you know what I cannot accept? There was yet another lie in your story. Well, there are lots of other lies in your story, but I'll get to them one at a time. You lied that your husband physically abused you. I cannot believe that he did all those horrible things to you. I don't think that he ever hit you. I say that with conviction because no one ever saw it. I just have your word for it. But now you'll say that you had visited that NGO several times and recounted all the physical abuse stories. That was a lie as well. No, visiting them wasn't a lie because that lie could have been easily unfurled. You definitely visited them. What you really did was cleverly create a false narrative that your husband was a violent man, and you used that NGO as supportive evidence. How could they really know if it was your husband who inflicted those wounds on you, or well . . . you know . . . you did it to yourself, didn't you?

'Every time you had an argument with your husband in front of other people, you'd go back to your room and injure yourself. Then the following day, insinuate that it was your husband who hit you. Do that over and over again and eventually people start believing you. Vicky, your helper Sharda, that woman at the NGO, they all believed you. Hell, even I believed you and felt sorry for you. I thought you were one of the countless women in this world who are persecuted and abused by their husbands. I was happy for you that you got rid of Anant, that the bastard got what he deserved. I had decided to do whatever I could to help you get a lenient sentence after you confessed. After all, I believed that you were a victim. And you killed your husband on the spur of the moment, without any premeditation.

'You've been a very crafty liar, I must admit. But what really gave you away was another of your lies. You think you're very smart, which you are, there is no question about that, but you proved to be too smart for your own good. Coming back to the specific words that you used in your statement, namely "provocation", "sudden", "grave", "self-control", "mistake", "accident". They are exactly by the book, more specifically, under exception 1 of section 300 of the Indian Penal Code. You know that, don't you? That Section 300 has five exceptions where culpable homicide does not amount to murder, thereby awarding a milder punishment. Of course you do. And you chose the first exception.

'You knew that the essentials of this exception are, and I quote verbatim from the Indian Penal Code, "that there must be a provocation. The provocation must be grave and sudden. By reason of such grave and sudden provocation, the offender must have been deprived of the power of self-control. The death of the person who gave provocation was by mistake or accidental."

'What really struck me as odd was why you kept using these specific words in your statement? And then it hit me. You had it planned all along. You wanted your crime to be considered under exception 1 of section 300. And why? Because the punishment under this crime is far milder than under a culpable homicide that amounts to murder which leads to life imprisonment. In fact, it was clear from your statement, and what you made us all believe, that you had no intention of killing your husband. Add to that the false narrative of physical abuse that you created, it was very likely that the court would have seen you as a victim as well and granted you a very light sentence. You could have even escaped with just a minor fine or with no punishment. And that is why you confessed. Everyone regards a convict, who is a victim of physical abuse, with lenience. I wouldn't have been surprised if you would have gone scot-free with no punishment at all. In fact, I would have rooted for that as well.

'Another reason the court would've had a soft spot for you was because you made a clean breast of the crime; although you did lie to us during the first round of questioning, but you still did confess. And that got me thinking as well. You knew that I had no hard evidence against you, that there were no witnesses to the crime, so why did you confess so easily? And why did you not erase your fingerprints from that vase?'

'Therein lies your genius. When something is so obvious, so apparent, we tend to disregard it. Since your fingerprints were not tampered with, we felt that you couldn't have been so stupid as to leave them behind after killing your husband. Even an amateur criminal would know that. But you purposely left them behind so we could have this line of thinking. You wanted us to believe that you were stupid. If you really wanted to show the crime as a mistake, it served you better to appear stupid in the eyes of the law and leave the fingerprints behind. That way, we wouldn't have suspected that you had an ulterior motive all along for the crime.

'But this was your, let's call it, plan B. In case you got caught, you would have gotten away with a minor punishment with the series of false narratives built into your story. But I think that was your back-up plan. Your primary plan, let's call it plan A, was your master plan. It was to pin the murder on someone else and get away with it completely. You would've thought that in case plan A failed, you should have a back-up, and so you had to create a pathetic and oppressed image for yourself as per your plan B.

'What was your plan A? That was a real stroke of genius. But before I figured that out, I had to dive into your back story. I had to figure out who you were, and that was when I realized that you weren't the ill-treated, bullied, poor slob of a woman that you wanted us to believe, but you're a strong, clever, die-hard feminist. You've always hated the notion of men lording over women and you are definitely not a woman who can easily be dominated by a man. That is why you left that job where the men ran the show and got that boy rusticated from your college. So, what happened?

'You must've hated your husband for telling you how to live your life. I'm guessing he went overboard the day of your first anniversary when he castigated you in front of your relatives. That might've been the day when you'd have decided that you couldn't take any more of his bullshit. But how could you just kill him and spend the rest of your life in prison? You *aren't* stupid. So, you planned and plotted. You planned for months and waited for the opportune moment to strike. You didn't let your impulses get the better of you. You waited. This was not a spur-of-the-moment crime. This was a well-planned, premeditated murder. You prepared for it for the better part of the last year. Am I right?

'Apart from waiting for the right moment, there was one more, very crucial, element in your plan. If there is a murder, there must be a killer. If you had to get away with it, you needed a scapegoat. Who better than your nincompoop brother-in-law? He *is* extremely stupid, and he doesn't even know what you did. You achieved the impossible. You poisoned the two brothers against each other. You polarized two affectionate brothers whose loving relationship was exemplified by their kith and kin. I think I know what you did.

'You started small and built it up from there. You sowed the seeds of discord without anyone suspecting you. Nothing obvious. Just a little nudge here and an inconsequential remark there, making Vicky commit and accept that Anant was indeed a domineering tyrant, controlling his life. And you did this repeatedly until he truly believed it. It's human nature to want to be consistent in our thought processes. If we don't like a certain person, chances are that, even if they don't wrong us, we'll continue to dislike the person because we've already formed an opinion about them. It gets difficult or, rather, inconvenient to change our mind. Consistency drives human action. You made Vicky take a stand and make a commitment that his brother was an overbearing bully. As soon as you succeeded with that, with regular nudges, you made sure that Vicky behaved consistently with that stand

and, eventually, he began quarrelling with his brother, something he had never had the gall to do before.

'Unfortunately for you, I'm a voracious reader and I devour books on history and psychology. Sometime ago I read that, during the Korean war, the Chinese communists used a similar strategy with the captured American soldiers—the Chinese asked them to make inconsequential anti-American or pro-Chinese statements. As these soldiers committed to their original statements, the Chinese then built it up from there with more substantive and significant remarks. The end result was that the American soldiers, unintentionally and unconsciously, turned against their country and became collaborators with the Chinese by sharing information and crucial military secrets. It all seemed trivial initially, but when sustained over long periods of time, the Chinese took advantage of this basic human tendency to remain consistent with our opinions.

'You deployed the same strategy. You psychologically assaulted your brother-in-law without his even knowing about it. You wanted the brothers to turn against each other. That was your strategy all along. You used Vicky as the scapegoat. You wanted him to be the prime suspect. You played your cards slowly and waited patiently. Opportunity arose in the form of that bookie. The bookie was your trump card. You knew Vicky was in need of a significant amount of money and it would infuriate Anant. You used that in your favour. Several months before that, you had already convinced Vicky to demand his share of the inheritance from his brother, with interest! You suggested he threaten Anant with legal proceedings, and even offered to provide Vicky with a lawyer. Boom! The conflict between the brothers exploded and they stopped talking to each other. The first stage of your plan A was successful. Now, if Anant were to die, sufficient suspicion would fall on Vicky.

'Now, with the bookie in the picture, the time was ripe. Vicky was in dire need of money, and he confessed to us that he had been desperate enough to physically fight his brother to wrest his rightful share of their inheritance from Anant. Who wouldn't have suspected Vicky of killing his brother? But what baffled me is why you killed Anant when Vicky wasn't home. Didn't that cripple your plan? The more I thought about it, the more I realized that you didn't plan to kill Anant that day. But you improvised. What really happened is that Mahesh visited Anant that night and you probably decided to capitalize on that fact and add one more suspect to confuse the police. If a crime cannot be solved due to insufficient evidence and contradictory statements, no one would be convicted. And you were fine with that. As long as you yourself weren't behind bars, you were fine with everything. But you made sure that Vicky called Anant just a few minutes before his murder. So, when the police checked the phone records, they saw Vicky's last call.

'You also timed the murder perfectly. You must have killed Anant right in the middle of the time window when Mahesh left and when Vicky would return home, to cast suspicion on both of them—Mahesh left your place at ten minutes past eleven, and Vicky returned home around half past midnight. You spoke to Vicky that night so you must've been aware when he'd be home. I'm guessing you might have killed Anant around ten minutes before midnight, which is bang in the middle of the time of the forensics' estimation of the time of the death.

'And to throw us off the scent even further, you had booked tickets to Dehradun that night before the murder for the following morning. Naturally, we assumed that if you killed your husband, you wouldn't be so stupid as to fly out the next morning. Again, same tactic. But then I realized that those flight tickets were just a pretence. You had no plans to go anywhere. In fact, I'm sure that you deliberately picked a fight with your husband that night in front of your helper. After killing Anant, you hit yourself to show us all the next day that your husband had assaulted you yet again. But that was for your plan B.

'To sum it up, this was a well-planned, premeditated and cold-blooded murder. You'd hit your husband with the murder weapon that night with every intention of killing him because you despised him. You entered his study under the pretence of having a conversation. You'd have decided early on that you'd use that vase for the strike as you couldn't have brought in a weapon from outside . . . that would jeopardize your plan B. Everything was calculated down to the last detail. Nothing was left to chance. After killing him, you did nothing. You simply walked to your room and slept as if nothing had happened. A dead body in the house did not perturb you. The next morning you woke up early to be consistent with your plan of flying out to Dehradun. And then you pretended to "discover" the dead body of your husband with your helper.

'But I think the biggest stroke of genius in your crime is that your brother-in-law is still clueless about what you managed to pull off. Vicky has no idea that he unwittingly collaborated with you at your will—by quarrelling with and being estranged from his brother—and that you planned to frame him for the murder. That nitwit still thinks that you are a great sister-in-law only wanting the best for him. It makes me laugh and cringe in horror at the same time. You're a psychotic and dangerous criminal who manipulates people. I will make sure that the judge throws the book at you when you are tried for culpable homicide leading to murder and awarded life imprisonment.

'Goodbye Mrs Kapoor.'